football shorts

stories chosen by
wendy cooling

Dolphin

A Dolphin paperback
First published in Great Britain in 1999
by Orion Children's Books
a division of the Orion Publishing Group Ltd
Orion House
5 Upper St Martin's Lane
London WC2H 9EA

Typeset by Deltatype Ltd, Birkenhead, Merseyside
Printed in Great Britain by Clays Ltd, St Ives plc

ISBN 1 85881 750 1

contents

first half

We didn't play like champions, but we fought like champions.

Manchester United manager Alex Ferguson

He makes you believe there is a football God after all.

Ron Atkinson on Ryan Giggs

If I wanted to be an individual I would play tennis.

Ruud Gullit who played with Feyenoord, AC Milan and Holland and went on to manage Chelsea and Newcastle United

lost ball
stops play

ALAN DURANT

We'd already thrashed them at our place. Twelve seven the score was, and it would have been thirteen if Chippy's trainer hadn't split and tripped him up with an open goal in front of him and not a Gordon Road Rover in sight. But would the Rovers accept their defeat? Would they shake hands like sportsmen and admit that the best team had won? That the Fairview Estate All Stars were the undisputed champions of Parkside and Gordon Road Rovers were rubbish? Would they heck.

'We can't play on concrete,' says Big Bennet. 'We play on grass. Anyway, concrete's not a proper football surface. Man United don't play on concrete, do they?'

'Man United play football,' sneers Kieron, or 'Incey' as we call him because he looks a bit like Paul Ince – well, from the back. Then Baby Bennet, Big Bennet's little brother, pipes up.

'We'd murder you at our place,' he says.

'You'd never,' says Natty. That's Natalie Peters, our striker.

'We would too,' Baby Bennet insists. And that's how come we're on Gordon Green this afternoon playing Gordon Road Rovers in a rematch.

It's a laugh, though, them calling this pitch grass. It's

got more bald patches than Chippy's dad and the grass that's there is brown and straggly. The only proper grass is down the sides where it's so long you could lose the ball in it. There's a massive great tree on the pitch too, half away along one of the sides.

'Call this a pitch,' grumbles Jumping Jack Roberts, our goalie.

'You can concede the match if you like,' says Brian Drain, 'Braindrain', their goalie, who knows every football rule in the book and a few that haven't been written yet. He wants to be a referee when he grows up, and he's already been on a couple of courses. Unfortunately he's not on one this afternoon.

'We're not conceding nothing,' says Incey fiercely. I don't reckon he knows what Braindrain's on about but anyway he doesn't like his tone.

'We can thrash you on any surface,' says Natalie and, noisily, we all agree.

'Come on, then,' says Big Bennet. 'Let's get started.'

The match is five-a-side and this is how the two teams line up:

Fairview Estate All Stars (hurrah!)
'Jumping Jack' Roberts
Sam Strong (me!)
Kieron 'Incey' Bishop
Li 'Chippy' Ho
Natty Peters

Gordon Road Rovers (boo, hiss!)
Brian 'Braindrain' Drain
Harry 'Crazy Horse' McNeil
Ivan 'Hacker' Hughes
Big Bennet
Baby Bennet

The game goes like a dream. Chippy and Natty
both hit hat-tricks, Kieron gets a couple and I score
one direct from a free kick. With a minute left, we're
nine four up and the Rovers are nowhere. We're on
the rampage, looking for that one goal that'll see us
into double figures when Braindrain strikes. He gets
to a long punt from Jumping Jack just ahead of Natty
and grabs the ball. Then he waves his team upfield.
That's not the way he faces, though. He turns sort of
sideways towards the big tree. Then he swings his foot
and gives the ball an almighty boot. We all look up as
the ball soars into the sky like a rocket powered
marshmallow. Up and up it goes. And it doesn't come
down – not to the ground anyway. It drops a little and
nestles neatly among the branches of the tree – a long
way up.

We stand for a moment or two, totally gob-
smacked.

'What you do that for?' says Incey eventually.

'Lost ball stops play,' says Braindrain smugly.

'But you did that on purpose,' says Natty.

'I can kick the ball wherever I like,' says Braindrain.

'And I can kick you wherever I like an' all,' says Jumping Jack who's come marching all the way up the pitch with a face like Monday morning.

'We'll have to call it a draw,' says Big Bennet with a shrug.

'A draw!' I say. 'You've got to be joking. We were murdering you.'

'That's the rules,' says Braindrain. 'If the ball is lost, then the game can't go on. That means the result's a draw.'

'A draw!' wails Incey. 'Never.'

Things look like they're going to turn as ugly as one of Hacker Hughes's slide tackles when Chippy raises a hand and says, 'Hey, guys, who says the game finished?' I'm just about to ask him where his ears have been hiding for the last few minutes, when he goes on, 'I can climb the tree, no problem. I get the ball.' We look at Chippy, then we look at the tree. Chippy's about three foot from head to toe and the tree's roughly ten miles high. Big Bennet laughs.

'You can't climb that,' he says.

'Sure, I can climb,' says Chippy with a grin. 'I climb chestnuts all the time.'

'It's not a chestnut tree actually,' says Braindrain smugly. 'It's a sycamore.'

'I'm sick of it all right,' Jumping Jack moans.

'No, no. I can climb. You see,' says Chippy confidently.

Then he's off. And, boy, can he climb! I've never seen Chippy's mum but I'm starting to think that maybe she's a mountain goat the way Chippy shins up that tree. In no time at all, he's half way up and the Gordon Road lot are looking sick as parrots. We, of course, are over the moon.

'Whoa! Go it, Chippy!' we shout. This is much more exciting than the match.

However … like the match, Chippy's climb comes to a sad and sudden conclusion.

Chippy's almost up to where the ball is lying when the branch he's standing on snaps. Chippy slips and down he drops. Luckily, though, his fall is broken by some leafy branches below and when we call up anxiously to see if he's okay there's a rustle of leaves and a round, very pale face peeks down at us.

'No problem,' Chippy says, but he doesn't sound half as cheerful as he did before he started climbing. 'I come down now,' he says meekly. There'd be no point in him going up again anyway – or any of the rest of us for that matter; the ball's out of reach now that branch has snapped off. Having looked a bit worried for a minute or so when Chippy was plumetting, Big Bennet is all grinny again now.

'That's it then, eh?' he says.

'Yeah, let's go home,' pipes his baby brother. Everyone's looking at me 'cause I'm the captain, but I

don't know what to say. No way do I want this game
to end like this, no way. What can I do, though?

'I've got an idea,' says Jumping Jack just as Chippy
reappears back on earth again, looking as floppy as a
fish in his Dad's shop before it goes in the fryer. 'Come
on,' says Jumping Jack to us.

'How do we know you'll come back?' says Hacker
Hughes suspiciously.

'Yes,' says Braindrain. 'If you all go, we can call off
the match you know. It's in the rules.' I give him a
look like in my opinion the name Drain is too good
for him; he should be called Sewer.

'It's okay,' says Chippy bravely. 'I stay.' And so it's
agreed.

'We're not waiting long, though,' Big Bennet calls,
as we follow Jumping Jack across the green.

Jumping Jack's idea is this: his mum's got a long pole
she uses to prop up her washing line; we borrow it and
use it to get the ball out of the tree. Sounds simple
enough. However, when we get to JJ's house and go
out into the garden, we discover two big problems:
one, the pole is at this moment holding up the entire
Roberts family weekly wash and, two, I don't reckon
it's nearly long enough anyway.

'Oi, Jack, are these yours?' says Incey with a grin,
pointing at a pair of horrible flowery knickers.

'Of course they're not,' says JJ hotly. 'They're my
sister's.'

'I don't care if they're your dog's,' I say. 'How are we supposed to get this pole? And anyway, it's too short.'

'It's not,' says JJ. 'It extends, doesn't it?'

'Great,' I say. 'But it seems to be a bit busy just now.'

'It's all right,' says JJ, 'we'll take it. The washing's nearly dry anyway.'

'Are you sure?' says Natty, eyeing up a soaking wet towel.

'Yeah,' says JJ and he goes over to the pole and starts to pull at it. It's not easy to get it away from the line and when he finally manages it with a massive tug, he falls flat on his back.

'Ow!' he cries as the pole clunks him a good one, right on the forehead. But there's no time to worry about that. We're all too busy taking in the disaster scene that was Jack's mum's high-flying washing line: towels and sheets are trailing in the flower beds; the odd sock has decided to make a leap for freedom; a bra is draped over Incey's head like earflaps ... And then there's this almighty, terrifying shriek.

'My washing! What's happened to my washing!' It's Jumping Jack's mum and she sounds like murder. We don't hang about. We turn and run.

'Great idea, Jack,' says Incey when we're safely out of murder distance. He's very image-conscious is Incey and it didn't do much for his image having a bra wrapped round his head.

'Well,' growls Jumping Jack, 'It wasn't my fault.

There wasn't any washing on the line when I went out, was there?'

'Hmmm,' says Incey. There's a deafening silence for a few moments like there was one minute to go in the Cup Final and our team had just gone a goal down. Then Natty speaks.

'Hey, guys,' she says, 'don't worry. It's okay, I've got an idea …'

Natty's idea is this: her dad's a window-cleaner and he's got lots of ladders, including one that's about a mile long (so Natty says); so we borrow one to get our ball down from the tree.

'Great!' we say, our spirits rising, our faces all smiles again, like our team just got the equaliser to take the match into extra time. Then we race round to Natty's.

This time, we decide, we'll ask first before we walk off with any ladder. Natty goes in the house to find her dad. But there's no sign of him and her mum's gone to the gym. Leaning against the front of the house, though, is the longest ladder I have ever seen. It would do the job, easy. The only problem is getting it down without causing terminal damage to ourselves, Natty's house, Natty's dad's van, plus anything and anybody else that happens to be in the street. We've got to go for it, though. It's too good an opportunity to miss. So, very carefully, we start to drag the ladder back. It weighs a ton, but eventually we manage to move it a bit. It scrapes along then sort of hops over the gutter and crashes against the wall underneath so hard that Natty and Kieron both fall over. Then the trouble begins.

'Oi! Who's mucking about with my ladder!'

We hear the angry voice of Natty's dad a moment before we see his (equally angry) face glaring down at us. He looks like an ogre who's just had his golden-egg-laying hen nicked. 'You kids!' he roars. 'What do you think you're doing?'

By the time we've apologised, explained, grovelled, and helped get the ladder back up where it was, we've wasted several precious minutes. For all we know the Gordon Road lot could be bidding Chippy a fond farewell at this very moment, but we can't give up. And, anyway, Incey's got an idea.

Incey's idea is this: we go and get his big brother. Incey's big for his age – he's head and shoulders above the rest of us – but his big brother Lynton's a giant. He's the best highjumper and basketball player in his school – in all the schools in the area. In fact, Incey tells us as we make our way round his house, Lynton may well be the best highjumper and basketball player in any school in the whole country. If the walk was much longer, he'd probably be the best high-jumper and basketball player in the entire universe.

'If anyone can get that ball down, Lynton can,' Incey says with total confidence.

The problem is Lynton won't. He's in the bath and he doesn't want to be disturbed.

'I just had a hard workout down the track, guys,' he says. 'Now leave me be, will you.'

'Hey, Lynton!' Incey shouts at the locked bathroom door. 'You've got to come. If we don't get that ball down, the match is a draw.' The immediate response is a loud slushing sound as Lynton settles himself in for a long wallow.

'So it's a draw,' he says finally. 'What's the problem. You win some, you lose some, you draw some. That's life.' This is rich, I reckon, coming from the best highjumper and basketball player in the universe. I mean, when did he last lose or draw? There's no point in hanging around any longer, though: Lynton's not coming and that's that.

There's only one option left. I don't like it, I'd never have suggested it. But, it's this or we don't get our win. And I want that win.

'We'll have to borrow Dan's ball,' I say grimly. Dan's my older brother. He's got a brilliant football he bought with his birthday money. He loves that ball; it's his favourite possession. He won't let me touch it. He won't even let me look at it. He's told me, several times, in great and gory detail, just what he'll do to me if he ever catches me so much as laying my little finger on it. He'd never lend it to me in a million years. Only, today he's gone fishing with Uncle Mike …

Mum's in the kitchen when we come in at the backdoor.

'Hi, Sam,' she says.

'Hi, Mum,' I say. Then, casually, 'Is Dan back yet?' Then she clocks Kieron and JJ standing behind me (we sent Natty back to Gordon Green to tell them we were on our way with a new ball). 'What are you lot up to?' she asks suspiciously.

'Oh, nothing,' I say, trying to sound airy as the breeze. 'We're just going to look at some stuff in my bedroom.'

'Oh,' says Mum. 'Well I'm just off out the front to pick some herbs.'

'OK,' I say. We follow her along the hallway then quickly climb the stairs. After that it's a cinch. We're in and out of Dan's room faster than you can say 'Ryan Giggs'. Then we speed down the stairs and head for the kitchen door … and that's when it all goes wrong – 'cause when I push the door open, who do I see sitting there but Uncle Mike and Dan. Luckily, Dan's got his back to me, but Uncle Mike's seen me so I can't go back. All I can do is pass the ball behind me and walk on in.

'Hi,' I say. 'You're back early. Had a good fish?'

'Terrific,' says Uncle Mike. 'Eh, Dan?'

'Yeah,' says Dan, not looking at me, grinning at Uncle Mike. 'I caught a seven pounder.'

'Wow! Great!' I say. 'A seven pounder! That's … big.' As I speak this garbage, I'm sort of shuffling across the kitchen towards the back door, with the others following behind. We're all squashed together like Siamese triplets, trying to hide the ball, which I can feel pushing into my back and have worked out must be nestling under JJ's jumper. It nearly works too. Nearly. I'm just a foot from the door and freedom when Uncle Mike stops us in our tracks.

'You've put on a bit of weight there, Jack, haven't you?' he says.

'Oh, yeah,' says JJ shakily. 'Yeah. Been eating a lot of cakes and stuff.'

Uncle Mike grins. 'It looks like you've swallowed a football,' he says and Dan laughs. I laugh too, a small forced laugh and so does Incey. JJ smiles sort of sheepishly as if he's just let in a soft goal. Then Dan stops laughing. His face clouds over like he's just found out his seven pounder was actually a large boot.

'If that's my football you've got there …' he growls. And that's that. The game's up. Over. The final whistle's been blown. We've lost.

We troop back to Gordon Green a defeated side. We've only been gone twenty minutes but it seems like a lifetime. All our efforts have been for nothing.

And, as if this wasn't bad enough, a big wind's got up and is trying to blow our heads off.

'There'll be another day,' Incey shouts over the wind. But that's no consolation. We want to beat those Gordon goons today.

'So you got here at last,' Big Bennet greets us. 'You think we've got nothing better to do than hang around in this wind waiting for you?'

'It was your goalie that kicked the ball in the tree remember,' says Jumping Jack grumpily.

'Yeah, well,' says Big Bennet. 'You got the ball or what?'

I glare at him. 'No,' I say eventually. 'We haven't.'

Big Bennet's face looks as happy as Christmas. 'That's it then,' he says. 'Game's over. It's a draw.'

'A draw,' Braindrain repeats, as if we needed to hear it a second time.

'We want a rematch,' says Kieron.

'Yeah, yeah,' says Big Bennet. 'We'll …'

We don't hear what they're going to do, though, because Big Bennet's words get lost in a roaring rush of wind that's so strong it nearly lifts Baby Bennet right off his feet.

It does something else too.

There's a heavy thud behind us and we all jump. Then

we turn to see what's fallen … It's the ball. The wind's brought down the ball! Half of us look at it like it's the winning lottery ticket, the other half like it's a bowl of cabbage stew. I don't have to tell you which is which.

'Right, then,' I say. 'Let's finish the match …'

The last minute is a massacre. Chippy, Natty and Incey each rattle in another goal just like that and the final score is 12–4. Not even Braindrain can find a way of wriggling out of this one. The Gordon Road Rovers have been beaten fair and square. Fairview Estate All Stars are the undisputed champions of Parkside!

'You know,' says Incey, as we stroll home in triumph, 'maybe we should play on grass all the time.' He grins. 'After all, Man United don't play on concrete, do they?'

the happy team

ALAN GIBBONS

We've always been a happy team. We had to be when you think about it. It's the names, you see. There's me for a start, Danny Merrie. Then there's my best mate, Mark Jolley. You think that's a bit of a coincidence? You ain't heard nothing yet. Our captain's the same. Pete Smiley, he's called. That's wily Smiley to his mates, on account of his grasp of soccer tactics.

My dad says it must be something in the water. How else would you get a Merrie, a Jolley and a Smiley in one school, never mind in one team?

Mum say's maybe it's the history of our area. It probably goes back to the Middle Ages or something. You know, like men in brown nightgowns and bald heads. Or plague pits. Yes, maybe our great-great-great-great grandparents were medieval comedians. Or, more likely still, village idiots!

Personally, I think it's all one big coincidence. Like the charity football competition. We couldn't believe it when the letter came round school. A local company was donating a cash prize to support junior sports. It was the answer to our prayers. It's Guppy, you see. His little sister was really ill. She was born ill, some tube inside her didn't work properly. And I don't mean sick-on-your-sheets ill, or kiss-it better ill. No, Ramila was in a bad way. Let's be honest, she was

dying. We all felt sorry for Guppy. He was great,
always cheerful and full of jokes. A proper Happy
Team member. He adored Ramila. We thought he was
weird sometimes. Most of us can't stand our little
brothers and sisters. Well, who wants something
round the house that's wet at both ends, screams a lot
and gets all the attention? But Guppy was proud of
his sister. She was brave. Brave the way a football is
round.

So the moment I saw the charity soccer competition letter pinned up outside the head's office I went
looking for Guppy.

'Seen this?' I asked.

Guppy took the letter and just stared at me. For a
moment I thought he was going to cry. But he didn't.
That would be too naff by half. His voice went really
low.

'For Ramila, you mean?'

'Of course for Ramila,' I told him. 'Five hundred
pounds to the winning team, it says. To be paid to a
charity of their choice. Well, I can't think of a better
cause than a dying kid, can you?'

'No.'

Guppy was excited. His family's been raising
money for months. Ramila's only got one chance.
There's this operation, but they don't do it in Britain.
She'll have to go to America and it will cost a fortune.
The people round our way have been amazing. All the
shops have got posters with Ramila's face on them,

and collecting tins. The black cabs are the same. They've got them up too. You get the odd idiot who scribbles things on the posters. You know, 'Paki' and rubbish like that, but most people are great. A sick kid's a sick kid in any language and that's all that matters. With the five hundred pounds prize money we would reach the target.

'Let's tell the lads,' said Guppy.

So we did.

They jumped at it, of course. That's the sort of team we are. All for one and one for all. Like I told you, happy. Well, except for Slammer. With him, it's more a case of all for me. On the quiet, I think he's the one who scribbled on Ramila's posters, but I'd decided not to let on to Guppy. Slammer's never fitted in properly. It's not that he can't play. No, he's a natural striker and he's got a good engine. Our manager, Tommy Dolan, thinks Slammer could even get a trial for Everton or Liverpool. But it's his personality that's wrong. He had a big fight with Guppy once. He wouldn't stop skitting him. That's why I didn't tell Guppy about the posters. Bad for team morale.

You could say Slammer finds it difficult to be a team player, and I'm putting it politely.

'Sounds stupid to me,' said Slammer, the moment we'd finished.

'Why's it stupid?' asked Mark.

'Well, why can't we keep the money ourselves?'

'Because it's to help other people, that's why,' said Mark.

Slammer frowned. There was only one sort of people he wanted to help – and that was himself.

Mark shook his head. He doesn't like Slammer, but then who does? If he wasn't our best player, he would have had the old heave-ho months ago.

'The whole thing's a waste of time, if you ask me,' said Slammer.

'Nobody *was* asking you,' Mark snapped.

Slammer just sulked, but then he always does, and while he sulked we made plans. After a bit of argy bargy the plans became one Master Plan, and it went something like this:

One   Post off the application form. (That was the easy bit).

Two   Hammer the opposition.

Three Hand the cheque over to Guppy's mum and dad.

Four   Wave Ramila off at the airport.

Not much of a Master Plan, you might think, but it suited us fine. All except Slammer. Just when we were all smiles (well, we are the Happy Team) he piped up, grumbling as usual.

'How come the money has to go to *his* family?' he demanded, nodding in Guppy's direction.

'Because,' Mark told him shortly, 'Guppy's the one with the sick sister.'

'Well, I don't think it's fair,' snorted Slammer.

'Look,' I said, noticing steam starting to come out of Mark's ears. 'Make your mind up, Slammer. Are you in or out?'

Slammer gave Guppy a sidelong glance. 'In,' he said after a long pause.

Somehow none of us liked the way he said it. A sly sort of grin came across his face. It was like he'd suddenly come up with his own Master Plan.

'What's with him?' asked Mark.

'Beats me,' I answered. 'Nothing to bother us, anyway.'

But I was wrong. Dead wrong, as we were soon to find out.

It was a fortnight before we got a reply to our application, but it was worth the wait.

'We're in!' Pete announced. 'Qualifying match this Saturday, then a knockout tournament the following week if we get through.'

'*If* we get through!' scoffed Mark. 'We'll walk it.'

He had good cause to be confident. We were running away with the North Liverpool Junior League. Our manager, Tommy Dolan, said we were unstoppable. On the back of five straight wins, we were leading the league by six clear points.

'A cup competition's a bit different, of course,' said Guppy.

'Yeah,' said Mark. 'We play the league for fun. This,' he waved the letter, 'this is for a mate.'

Everybody started digging Guppy in the ribs and messing his hair. He looked embarrassed. But happy.

That's when I noticed Slammer out of the corner of my eye. He was staring. Just staring at Guppy. Like he was his worst enemy. Right away I was thinking about how Slammer had grinned, and the way we all thought he'd written on the posters and I found myself wondering if Mark wasn't getting just a bit too confident.

As it turned out, I was worrying over nothing. When Saturday came round, we were up against this outfit called Croxteth Celtic. It wasn't easy, but we kept our nerve. They flew at us right from the kick-off. Mad, they were.

We'd already had a couple of scares when they got a free kick on the edge of the box. Well, this lanky kid lollops up and hits a screamer of a free kick. Mark was in the wall and it was going straight at him until he ducked. It cannoned off the bar with a tremendous crack.

'You ducked,' screamed Pete. 'There's no point in being part of the wall if you get out of the way of the ball. What did you duck for?'

'If I hadn't,' Mark retorted irritably, 'it would have taken my rotten head off.'

That was the last time they had us rattled though, the team *and* the crossbar. Celtic tired after that and we eventually ran out 4–1 winners. Guppy and Pete scored, but Slammer was our man of the match again.

He scored two and made both the others. No wonder
he walked off smiling. The trouble is, I couldn't help
wondering if he didn't have something else on his
mind beside his brace of goals. Mark and Pete
reckoned I was worrying about nothing, but I wasn't
so sure. If you'd seen the way Slammer was grinning,
you'd know what I mean. We're talking crocodiles.

'Three more wins,' said Mark on the way home,
'and Ramila's off to the States.'

'And the way Slammer's playing,' Pete chimed in,
'we're a dead cert.'

Though I didn't let on, this funny idea kept rattling
round in my brain. What if Slammer stopped playing?

By the following Saturday, I'd almost forgotten
about my suspicions. It was the excitement, I suppose. For a start, Guppy's dad had been in touch with
the hospital in America. They could do the operation
within a month. They just needed the money.

'Do you think we can do it?' asked Guppy as we got
changed.

'Think?' said Mark. 'I *know*.'

'Tell you what,' said Pete, glancing at the changing-
room clock. 'Old Slammer's cutting it fine.' 'Yes,' said
Guppy. 'He is, isn't he?'

Cutting it fine was an understatement. As we
clattered out of the changing-room we looked up and
down the road. No Slammer. As we jogged onto the
pitch we gave a last look round. Still no Slammer.

'You'd think he could have phoned,' Pete complained. 'He's only our star player.'

'Forget it,' said Mark. 'Tell Gerry Jones to get his tackle off. We'll have to use our sub. Slammer or no Slammer, we're going to win this.'

A couple of words went unspoken. For Ramila. But Mark would never have said anything that soppy.

I glanced at the other quarter-finals taking place on the other pitches. So this was Slammer's plan. Stay away and hope we lose. Somehow, I felt relieved. I'd expected a lot worse from him.

Slammer's absence didn't make much difference in the first match. We hammered our opponents 6–3. The semi-final was tougher though. We had to come back from behind twice and at full time it was all square, 2–2.

'Penalty shootout,' grumbled Tommy Dolan. 'And we're lucky to be in that. We're missing Slammer.'

But not when it came to penalties. We converted every one. The only trouble is, so did the other side.

'Miss it,' whispered Guppy as their fourth penalty-taker placed the ball.

I smiled. It wasn't like Guppy to wish ill on anyone, but I suppose this was an exception.

'Please miss it,' Guppy whispered.

The lad did too. By a mile.

'You certainly put the mockers on him,' said Pete.

'Yes,' said Guppy with a smile. 'I did, didn't I?'

He glanced at his mum and dad standing on the

touch-line with Ramila. It looked like the dream was coming true.

Mark slotted home his penalty. Another miss by the opposition and we were home and dry.

'Got the evil eye ready, Guppy?' I asked.

Guppy smiled. Quietly. But when the penalty-taker spooned it over the bar he roared. Loudly.

'That's it,' said Pete. 'We're in the final. Come on, the other semi is still playing. Let's see who we're up against.'

As we walked across the playing field we were smiling from ear to ear. That's when we spotted him.

'Slammer!'

The smiles vanished.

'Where?'

'There.'

'The traitor,' said Mark, clenching his fists. 'The rotten traitor. Who's that he's playing for?'

'Stoneycroft Rovers,' Tommy Dolan told us. 'I've been watching them. They're a useful outfit.'

Useful was right. Just before the final whistle Slammer stuck a cracking volley. It was the winner: 4–3.

As Slammer came off, Pete had a go at him. 'This is a dirty trick. You know how much this means to Guppy.'

Slammer gave a low, throaty chuckle. 'Yes. Why do you think I did it? You're going to get buried.'

'That's it, then,' groaned Guppy. 'We've had it.'

'No we haven't,' said Pete.

'But he was our best player. Now they've got him.'

'So we reorganise,' said Pete. 'Somebody's got to mark him out of the game.'

'That means me,' said Mark. 'Get it? Mark the marker.'

But come the final, Mark the marker was Mark the muffer. We were two-nil down in ten minutes. Slammer made one and scored one. The dream was fading fast.

'Enjoying the match?' gloated Slammer as he jogged past.

We just turned away.

'We're getting roasted,' Pete complained as he retrieved the ball from our net. 'And it's all down to Slammer.'

I saw him looking at us. I saw the grin.

'Maybe Mark's the wrong person to put on Slammer,' I murmured.

'So who?'

'Somebody with more reason to stop him,' I said. 'Guppy.'

'Guppy?' said Pete. 'But tackling's not his game.'

'It is now,' I told him.

'Meaning?'

'Meaning. I know who scribbled on the posters.'

Guppy looked across the pitch. 'You mean?'

'Yeah, Slammer.'

From the re-start Stoneycroft came at us again.

Slammer picked up the ball in the channels and surged forward. But it had become a grudge match. Guppy was tackling like a Rottweiler.

'Nice one,' said Mark.

A minute later Slammer had it again. But Guppy got in his tackle. Like a Pit Bull. We watched Slammer rising gingerly to his feet. The grin had vanished.

Next time Slammer got the ball he just pushed it away. Before Guppy could even tackle.

'Now we can make a game of it,' said Pete.

Mark was happier in attack than man-to-man marking. He picked the ball up on the left and drove into the box. Determined to make up for losing out in the duel with Guppy, Slammer came in hard.

'Penalty!'

Mark placed the ball. With a short run-up he side-footed it to the goalie's left: 2–1.

Tommy Dolan was on the touch-line, holding up five fingers. As we laid siege to their area, Stoneycroft brought every man back. Twice, we had shots scrambled off the line. I glanced at the touch-line. Tommy Dolan was gesturing. Three fingers. Three minutes.

Guppy had the ball on the edge of the area, jinking and dribbling.

'Square,' shouted Pete suddenly. 'Across the box.'

Guppy didn't even look up. He just back-heeled it. Pete stuck it hard and low. I knew it was coming my way so I stuck out a foot. It could have gone anywhere. But it deflected into the net: 2–2.

Suddenly Slammer was sweating. And not because of the running he was doing. His side was rocking on its heels. In less than thirty seconds we were pinning them back in their own half again. Pete hit the post and I had a shot palmed over the bar. I glanced at Tommy Dolan. He was drawing his index finger across his throat. The ref was going to blow any moment.

'I don't fancy another penalty shoot-out,' said Pete. 'Everybody up for the corner.'

As it came over I leapt, but it was too high. I was dropping back to the ground when I saw somebody coming in on my left. Guppy. He got right over the ball and headed it down: 3–2.

The ref didn't even get to blow the whistle. We'd won. I didn't even see Slammer after that. But I knew for certain the grin was gone for good. There isn't much more to tell, really. Ramila had the operation and she's well on the mend. So much so that Guppy's even started saying what a pain she is! As for the team, we went on to win the league.

Now that's what I call a happy team!

goalkeeping? easy!

MICHAEL HARDCASTLE

Andy Bourne was bouncing the ball on the goal-line and then throwing it to team-mates who tried to beat him with a header.

'Easiest job in the world, that,' scoffed Travis Jarman after seeing Andy catch his close-range shot. 'Anybody can do it.'

'Rubbish!' Andy fired back at him. 'A goalie's got to be really talented in all sorts of ways that you'd never even think of. All you do is stick the ball in the net when you get the chance. *And* you've got other strikers to help you. I'm always on my own, the very last line of defence. You'd get bored on your own, Trav. You'd lose concentration.'

'No I wouldn't! Listen, I played in goal loads of times before I became a top striker. So I know I'm good.'

'That's enough, you two,' said George Banner, captain of Faxenby Flyers, their team. 'We're supposed to be practising our skills for the game against Colombard, not arguing with each other. Whatever happened to our team spirit?'

Moments before the Colombard match was due to kick off Andy Bourne was missing.

'You know, I think it's deliberate,' said Jonathan. 'He wants Travis to prove his boasts about being a good goalie.'

'Oh, I don't think so,' said George. 'Andy's too loyal to let us down like that. He loves keeping goal, so he wouldn't miss a game unless he was ill or injured. I'll get one of the parents over there to ring him.' He turned to Travis. 'Trav, we need a goalie now, so how about it? I mean, I can get Gary, the sub, to take your place up front. He'd be useless in goal. Too small, to start with.'

'Yeah, sure, be glad to star between the posts,' Travis said enthusiastically, much to George's surprise. 'Andy will never get his place back after my performance.'

'Just don't let us down, that's all,' warned George. 'Colombard are not a bad side. Decent defenders, anyway.'

'Well, if you need goals from me I'll switch back to striker easily,' Travis offered.

'No way!' said George firmly. 'You're our goalie now, so your job is to prevent goals, not score 'em!'

News that Faxenby were playing an inexperienced goalkeeper soon spread. Colombard began to hit shots from every range but Travis dealt confidently with all of them. Yelling encouragement to his fellow defenders, he pointed out that they could pass the ball back to him whenever they liked. Up front, Faxenby were not playing well against a tall, steady defence. Gary could never win the ball in the air and he fluffed a couple of easy chances in the box.

'I'd've put those away before their goalie could

even blink,' claimed Travis, dancing up and down
with annoyance. His team-mates didn't doubt that
but knew he had to stay where he was.

Suddenly, a Colombard striker broke through with
the ball at his feet and only one defender and Travis to
beat. The defender chased after him, launched a
sliding tackle and brought him crashing to the
ground. It had to be a penalty. Travis tried to protest
but the ref wouldn't listen. Now, Travis knew, he
would be tested to the full.

Colombard's stocky captain strode up, put the ball
on the spot and fired it powerfully towards the roof of
the net. Travis hadn't moved a millimetre before the
ball was kicked, so when it flew almost straight at him
all he had to do was jump and, with one hand, tip it
over the bar. He'd saved his first penalty! As the team
gathered in the box for the corner kick most said
'Great save!' and patted him on the back. Travis
looked smug. After all, he hadn't expected to be
beaten. What's more, he nonchalantly jumped out to
take the ball from the corner kick and punt it up-field.
Life for a goalie, he was deciding, was far easier than
life for a striker.

A few minutes later he was changing his mind.
Jonathan, attempting a clearance in a crowded goalmouth, miskicked completely. The ball sliced
upwards and then the spin turned it towards the net.
Although taken by surprise, Travis leapt sideways and
almost managed to get a hand to it. But it was

impossible to prevent it dropping just inside the post for a calamitous own goal.

'You maniac!' Travis yelled at the culprit.

'Sorry, sorry, sorry!' apologised Jonathan, his face as scarlet as his Faxenby shirt.

'Better go down on your knees to George, he'll never forgive you,' said Dale, a fellow defender.

George, however, soon had something to celebrate. For, as if to match Faxenby in style, Colombard also conceded an own goal in bizarre circumstances.

Gary, desperate to keep his place as a striker, charged in from the left wing and fired the ball furiously into the box in the hope that someone would get to it. The only player who did was the Colombard sweeper. Confident he knew where his goalkeeper was, he trapped the ball and in the same movement turned it sideways for his keeper to clear. But the goalie had moved in another direction and he watched helplessly as the ball trickled over the goal-line. Gary wanted to claim it but George wouldn't allow that.

'Just be thankful we're on level terms,' he said. 'We haven't played well enough to get a point.'

That was how the match ended. In the dressing-room Travis asked about Andy Bourne.

'Damaged his ankle, falling off something, according to his mum when Mr Peel rang her,' George reported. 'Don't know if he'll be fit for the Beldock game but you seemed to manage okay. Better than I expected, actually.'

'*Told* you I was good,' Trav responded, irritated that his captain hadn't believed him or praised him sufficiently. 'But I'd've scored a hatful today if I'd been up-front. Gary should shoot himself for missing so many.'

When he set out to visit Andy that evening Travis still wasn't sure whether he really wanted to continue keeping goal, but after all he'd said to Andy and George he knew he couldn't admit that publicly. So much would depend on Andy's health.

Things definitely didn't look good when Mrs Bourne ushered him into the sitting-room. For Andy was reclining on the sofa, his legs bare and his right ankle not only heavily strapped but also packed in ice.

'You haven't moved, have you?' his mother demanded sharply. 'How can I?' enquired Andy. He glanced at Travis and seemed as embarrassed as Jonathan was at scoring an own goal.

'You haven't broken it, have you?' Travis asked anxiously, handing over some chocolate he'd brought to share with his injured team-mate. Andy shook his head.

'Just sprained the ligaments or something like that. The ice is getting the swelling down. Wish I hadn't done it. The pain was terrible.'

'So how'd you do it?' Travis wanted to know.

'Swinging from a swing,' said Andy. 'I mean, there wasn't a seat in it, just a frame. I was moving on it like –'

'– like a monkey?' laughed Travis.

'Like a monkey, indeed,' agreed Mrs Bourne, coming in at that moment. 'He does it from door frames, too, and it's got to stop. His arms are quite long enough, thank you. No more, Andrew, or it'll be the end of football for you *for ever*!'

'I do it to *strengthen* my arms, not just lengthen them,' he protested, but his mother, after cuffing a cushion or two, had gone again. He looked at Travis for understanding and Travis, a believer in total fitness himself, nodded. 'I mean, I want to go right to the top as a goalie, so I've got to be brilliant. *Now*. I just wish our defence didn't keep letting me down by giving away stupid goals. Players like Dale make me really mad. He doesn't listen to what I tell him and he doesn't talk to the rest of the defence when he should do. You know, *warn* them what's happening. People can't see out of the back of their heads, can they?'

'Yeah, I know just what you mean,' Travis said. 'Same thing happened today with Jonathan. Took his eye off the ball and sliced it into our own net. Crazy! Gave me no chance of a save and cost us three points. Well, two, because we did get a draw. Made me so mad!'

'But you wouldn't get blamed for that, Trav,

because you're not the real goalkeeper. If I do the slightest thing wrong, though, I get all the blame. Goalies are always a soft target for abuse, I can tell you. Our mistakes are never forgiven.'

Travis nodded again. He was thinking about the praise that goalies sometimes got for making out-of-this-world saves; somehow that didn't compare with the adulation heaped on the scorer of a winning goal in a Cup-tie or a top-of-the-table clash.

'When do you think you'll be back in action, Andy?' he asked.

'No idea,' said Andy gloomily. 'The doc says I've got to rest up my ankle for a bit before I try to run. And Mum is threatening to keep me off football for good because she says it's dangerous. She's said that before and usually I get her to change her mind. *Usually*. But she thinks this is a dire injury.'

'So I expect I'll be in goal for the Beldock game, then,' said Travis.

'Bound to be. But you said you like it!' Andy pointed out. 'And you didn't let in a goal, did you? Well, not a real one. With me on the injured list George needs you.'

After a brief discussion about the prospects for the match against one of the League's toughest teams Travis left. At home he watched a video of one of his heroes in action and thought about his own future.

'You okay?' his mum asked him. 'Never known you so quiet.'

'Got a lot on my mind,' Travis confessed.

'Well, if it's about football, stop worrying,' said his mum. 'Everybody says you're very good at what you do – or so I'm told.'

'Right,' said Travis. 'But *what* do I do?' He didn't expect an answer and he didn't get one.

Beldock Bees were known, predictably, as the Stingers and they enjoyed their reputation of being an all-action side with a fondness for the counter-attack. If they went a goal down their supporters expected them to hit back immediately; and invariably they did, no matter how well their opponents defended.

'Our plan must be to attack *them* continuously,' said George before the kick-off. 'That way we'll also be protecting our keeper and –'

'I don't *need* protecting!' Travis interrupted indignantly. 'I can take care of myself. Nobody'll get the ball past me, not even one of *our* defenders.' He couldn't help shooting a glance at Jonathan but Jonathan just shrugged. He knew he didn't make a habit of scoring own goals.

Travis was wearing a new black sweater so that the colour didn't clash with the yellow of their opponents' shirts and the scarlet of Faxenby. He felt it made him stand out against everyone else and that, somehow, increased his confidence.

In the opening minutes of the match, however, he wished he was at the other end of the pitch. That was

where the action was. Faxenby were faithfully following George's orders to attack and they swarmed
around the Bees' goalmouth. Two or three times it
seemed they must score but chances were missed
through over-eagerness until at last Gary forced the
ball over the line in a desperate scramble for possession. He was ecstatic. It was his first goal for the Flyers,
and it was the happiest moment of his life. Travis
signalled his congratulations but he knew he himself
would have scored long before this if he'd been
leading the attack.

Of course, Beldock tried to hit back immediately,
only to find that the Faxenby midfield still had a firm
grip and were letting nothing escape them. Then the
Bees changed their tactics and began to hit long balls
for their twin strikers to chase.

Dale and Jonathan and the rest of the defence were
soon under real pressure. But they were coping well
and Travis hadn't had a single shot to save until the
Bees' nippy, redhaired striker suddenly broke clear
with only the goalkeeper to beat. Travis didn't
hesitate. He dashed out, prepared to dive at the
attacker's feet for the ball. As Travis went down the
Beldock player tried to swerve round him, only to
stumble. Then, in his eagerness to recover the ball
which Travis managed to grab with one hand, he
stepped on Travis's arm and then fell. In his rage and
pain Travis hurled the ball at him as his opponent was

getting to his feet. Promptly, the boy went down again.

'You really deserve a red card for that but I hate to send a schoolboy off!' snapped the referee. 'If you display the same violence again I shan't hesitate to dismiss you, so be warned.'

Travis took his time receiving treatment from the parent acting as the team's physio, because he knew the penalty couldn't be taken until he was ready to face the kick. The delay, he hoped, might put the kicker off. Unhappily for Faxenby, it didn't. This time Travis was given no chance to make a save as the ball whistled into the corner of the net. The Stingers had stung: the teams were level again. Travis nursed his arm and cursed his luck. None of his team-mates said 'Bad luck!' to him or anything like that. Plainly, they felt he was to blame for Beldock's goal. George, especially, looked really upset.

After that success, the Stingers kept up the momentum of their attacks, determined to take the lead. Travis was too busy to think about the pain in his arm. In any case, it didn't hinder his handling of the ball. An attacker who tried to bundle him over as a corner-kick was taken was fiercely rebuked by Travis.

'You've got a mouth as big as a goalmouth!' his opponent jeered. Travis felt like hitting him. He didn't know that the boy used the same phrase to wind up every goalie he met; he had a theory that the insult would infuriate them and they'd lose concentration and make mistakes. Sometimes it worked. But this time Travis's skills were not undermined and he remained in command of his net.

At half-time, however, George had a word with him.

'Look, whatever you do, stay cool. Don't get another card. We can't afford to have our goalie sent off. We'd have no chance against this lot with only ten men. There's nobody else I could trust between the posts.'

Travis nodded, pleased with the compliment but wishing it had been warmer. He remembered Andy's view of the treatment goalkeepers usually received from team-mates and spectators.

'Don't worry, skipper, I'll keep my temper and I'll keep a clean sheet from now on. I mean, they won't get another penalty, will they?'

But they did. Well into the second half Dale was involved in a tussle for the ball with an attacker on the edge of the box. The striker turned this way and that, trying to outwit Dale, but Dale stuck with him and then, stretching his foot out for the ball, pushed his opponent over. The ref blew and pointed to the spot, a harsh decision by any standards.

'Oh no, Ref, it can't be!' Travis protested. But then he had the sense to fall silent when the ref glared at him. Travis now had to work out where the kicker would hit his shot. He was the boy fouled by Dale, not the one who'd taken the previous kick.

The kicker ran in, let fly – and Travis completely lost sight of the ball. Instead, he grabbed at the object sailing towards him – and found himself holding a boot! The cheers of the Beldock spectators told him the ball had landed in the net but the astonishment on the face of the kicker matched Travis's.

'But it's a goal, isn't it?' the boy asked anxiously. 'I mean, my boot must have come loose when I was fouled.'

'Can't be a goal, I never saw the ball and I was hit by this stupid boot!' Travis hurled it to the ground where it was gratefully seized by the owner. The ref was talking things over with a linesman and they concluded no rule had been broken: the goal stood.

'Honestly, goalies have to cope with idiots!' Travis raged. 'If I'd been taking a penalty I'd've made sure my boots were properly fastened on. Honestly, it should never have been a goal ...'

Nobody was listening because the game had resumed and the Stingers were going all out for a third goal to clinch victory. There looked to be no hope of Faxenby getting the equaliser. Then, during a brief stoppage, George dashed over to Travis, tugging at his left ear, always a sign he'd made a decision.

'Let's have your jersey because I want you up front again,' he ordered. 'Can't risk having you sent off and

I can see you're in the mood for a row. I'll take over. So you go and get us a goal, Trav.'

Travis thought of arguing and then changed his mind. Silently he handed over his black jersey and slipped on George's red shirt. After all, he knew he was getting what he really wanted. 'Good luck, skipper,' he said, and ran to join up with the attack in place of Gary who'd dropped back to fill George's place in midfield.

Full of energy, Travis ran at the opposition whenever he could get hold of the ball. He yelled for it, demanded it, pleaded for it. Beldock were awed by his pace and determination and their defence fell back, deeper and deeper. With five minutes of the match left, he made a goal for Gary who'd rushed forward to join in the hunt for the equaliser. And Gary took his chance neatly, slipping the ball past two defenders and then toe-poking it into the net.

Travis wasn't finished. He wanted victory. In the final minute, with the Bees helpless to stop him, Faxenby's top striker skipped over two desperate lunging tackles, slid the ball sideways to Gary and then screamed for its return. Gary obeyed. And Travis, swerving to his left and then to his right, lashed the ball beyond the goalkeeper's reach into the top of the net.

The match-winner disappeared under the piling bodies of his team-mates. It was, he knew, one of the best goals he'd ever scored. It was all he ever wanted to do.

'Nothing in the world is as good, as *glorious*, as getting a goal like that,' he told George when at last he could get to his feet. 'So you'd better make sure Andy's back between the posts for our next game. I'm staying up front.'

'Agreed,' grinned George, tugging at his left ear.

ugly me

ALAN BROWN

'm so ugly birds fall out of the sky when I look up at 'em. Milk turns sour on doorsteps as I go by. When I'm keeper the other football team can't score a goal. They see me and their shots go wide. It's all because I'm so ugly.

'You must be the ugliest person in the world,' says my mate Rich. I don't care, but I punch him anyway. Me and Rich, we're fighting friends. Sometimes I win and sometimes he wins. We don't hurt each other, much. That's what fighting friends are for.

Rich's got a twin sister called Abby. I never fight with Abby. She's beautiful, like a princess. When she's there all my words come out wrong, as if my tongue's too big for my mouth. I get clumsy, and drop things. I don't drop a thing when I'm in goal. Sticky Fingers, they call me.

'Hey, Sticky, we playing tonight?'

That was Tom. He's in my team. We don't have captains or anything – they just do what I say.

I can't sit still when we've got a game after school. Today I tried to make the teacher's writing fall off the blackboard by staring at it ever so hard. The words didn't fall off, but they did get a bit fuzzy. I felt Abby looking at me so I hid behind my desk lid.

On the way to the rec I started a traffic jam with ugly-vision. I made all the cars conk out. You can do that sort of thing when you're as ugly as me, and nobody ever knows it was you. It doesn't work on buses and lorries. That's 'cos they're diesels.

We had to wait for Rich because he'd got the ball. Danny and me had a fight, just to pass the time. I was doing all right until he punched me on the nose. It made my eyes water and the other kids thought I was crying, but I wasn't.

My nose felt like it was broken, but Danny got me to wobble it from side to side and said it was all right. He wouldn't have wobbled his nose from side to side when it felt like it was broken.

When I could see again Rich was there. With the ball – and Abby.

'Woo boo doin 'ere?' I couldn't talk too good, at first.

'I want to play,' she said.

I looked round the team. They all looked the other way. I looked at Rich. He shrugged and started digging holes in the pitch with his toe.

I got my voice back. 'You want to play?' was all I could say.

Abby laughed. 'There's no need to cry about it,' she said.

'I'm not crying!' I yelled. She was making me all hot and confused again.

'I want to play,' she repeated.

'Why?'

'Why not?'

'That's not a good answer.'

'It wasn't a good question.'

Rich and Danny started to kick the ball about. Tom joined in.

'We don't have girls in our team,' I said. The ball came to a rest at Abby's feet. 'They're not good enough.'

Abby spun the ball backwards, flicked it up and juggled it on her feet and knees. Then she trapped it, dribbled round me faster than I could turn and lobbed it over my head to Rich. He grinned.

Abby ran off to join in the game. I needed to fight somebody, but there wasn't anybody left.

Danny picked one team and I picked the other. I wanted Rich on my side so I had to choose Abby as well. I thought that Danny would pick her first, but he chose all his friends like he always does.

By half-time we were four nil up. Abby scored three and Rich got one. I was bored. Nobody made me dive, and a goalie's not tested unless they have to dive. That's what I like best.

Danny groaned. 'Hey, Sticky. Have mercy. Give us a player to even things up a bit.'

'Who do you want?' I asked. We both knew who was the best player. I wanted to see whether he would ask for her.

Danny hesitated and Abby spoke for herself.

'I'll swop,' she said, going over to the other side. She had a look in her eye that said 'Look out!'

I got all the diving I wanted, and more.

Abby got one past me, and then two. She did banana shots, volleys and diving headers. By the time she got her third I was so tired that even Danny put one in our net.

With five minutes to go we were even at four all. Then Rich scrambled another and put us ahead again.

The shots came at me from all directions. I dived this way and that. I was half kicked to death. My sticky fingers kept snagging the ball, but I was slowing down.

I booted the ball up field to get a breather. When it came back I was still panting. Abby beat my defenders. Her foot went back for the shot. It was me against her.

Abby's foot came forward and I dived to cover the near post. Her shot went like a bullet towards the other side of the goal. I lay in the mud and watched helplessly. The ball sped over the crossbar!

'The ref must be a friend of yours!' Danny shouted.

Tom was blowing the whistle. We'd won five four!

Danny ranted and raved. I laughed. So did Abby.

I felt really good as I walked home. Just one thing bothered me. Why had Abby laughed? Surely she wanted to win?

The next day at school the game was big news. Danny was still moaning, but everyone else had enjoyed it.

'Hello, Sticky.'

....

I nodded, dumb again.

'You're a good keeper,' she said.

'You're a great player, Abby,' I croaked.

'Where're you sitting?'

Did I say that, or was it her? I was getting flustered again. Danny and his cronies started poking fun, so I had to sort them out. Boys in our class don't talk to girls.

By the time Mr Hawkins arrived I was back in my seat next to Simon Bates. Abby sat on her own. She smiled at me and I smiled back, rubbing my knuckles. What a nice day.

'When did Abby start sitting on her own, Rich?'

Rich laughed at me. I didn't hit him straight away, seeing he's Abby's brother. 'She used to sit with Nazzam who went home to Pakistan,' he said. 'Why?'

'Nothing.'

Rich laughed again. 'That's what Abby said. She was asking about you.'

We had a good fight.

The next day I went over to Abby's desk.

'Could I sit here for a bit? I'm not sitting with Simon any more.'

'Have you been fighting?' she asked.

'No, not exactly.'

'I don't want you here if you're fighting all the time.'

My pride wouldn't let me go back to Simon. 'All right,' I said.

Abby smiled and the sun shone. 'I'd like that then,' she said.

Mr Hawkins said it was all right to sit with Abby, but it was going to be hard to keep my promise not to fight. Boys in our class don't sit next to girls.

'Who's Prince Charming?' Danny taunted. He's so dumb I don't even mind.

'Prince Charming.'

It was like an echo. I glared round to see who it was – Simon. So he was palling up with Danny. I rubbed my knuckles and they put their desk lids up and giggled.

They kept it up all day. It was more fun than lessons. Trilling 'Prince Charming, Prince Charming' like demented budgies.

I gave them ugly looks. They should have been terrified. They just laughed.

'Don't take any notice, Sticky,' said Abby.

Don't take any notice! It wasn't her they were laughing at. I used ugly-vision to make their hearts conk out. It didn't work. They must be diesels.

Next day I was early at school. Abby was late. It was just as well. Somebody had written 'Sticky loves Abby' on the board in the middle of a big red heart.

I knew who. Simon rubbed it off. Danny was a bit more stubborn. We were rolling on the floor when Abby came into the classroom.

'Sticky! You promised!'

'They said …'

'I don't care. You know what I said.'

My heart sank. 'You can't mean it.'

'Give me a good reason why not.' She folded her arms.

'There's nowhere to go,' I said desperately.

'There's plenty of spare desks at the back.'

'Everybody will laugh.'

'Let them laugh,' she said, and gave me that aggressive look again.

'Mr Hawkins wouldn't like it.' I'd hit on the right thing to say. It seemed to count with Abby.

She chewed her lip. 'Oh, all right,' she agreed. 'Just this once.'

I didn't want to sit with her when she was bossy like that. The fighting was all for her anyway.

In a rage I grabbed my books. I went to the back and scorched swear words into the desk lid with ugly-vision.

At playtime Abby wouldn't talk to me. She was surrounded by girl friends and they hissed like geese when I went near. Rich and me had a real fight. We were sent to the head teacher. She gave me a letter to take home to Mum. What a terrible day.

I raced to the rec and didn't even stop to make traffic jams. They must have thought it was Sunday.

The others strolled up in ones and twos. I tried to get them organised, but we were waiting for Rich and the ball again.

'You took your time.'

Rich wouldn't look at me. 'There were things to sort out,' he said.

'Well, let's get started,' I said. 'Who's going to choose?'

'Danny,' said Rich. Danny smiled. 'And Abby.'

'Hang on, we can't have two captains and I always choose.'

Now Rich looked at me. 'That's it, Sticky,' he said. 'We don't see why you should always choose.'

'Because I'm the best, that's why.'

'But you're only the goalkeeper, and Abby put three past you yesterday.'

'Only the goalkeeper, who says I'm only the goalkeeper?' I was getting into a fighting rage.

'I do, Sticky,' said Abby. 'Are you going to fight me?'

Everyone was against me. It hurt, but I gave in. At least I wouldn't have to wait long to get picked.

I waited, and waited. Players with two left feet were picked while I stood there with my face burning. Didn't they want a goalie? Under my breath I chanted, Choose me, Abby, choose me!

Danny finally picked me. I ran towards the goal – but John Harrison was already there.

'John wants a go in goal,' said Danny. 'We think that's fair.'

Fair! It might have been fair, but it wasn't football. Abby scored whenever she wanted against John Harrison. At half-time Danny grudgingly put me in goal. We lost eight two.

School next day was quiet. Nobody talked about the game. I don't think anyone had enjoyed it. Just before lunch Mr Hawkins called me to the front.

'What did your mother say about the letter?'

'Letter?'

'The letter, Sticky. The letter the head gave you to take home yesterday.'

I had forgotten the letter, lost the letter – my mind was completely blank about letters.

'At lunch, Sticky.' Mr Hawkins spoke with exaggerated patience. 'Find-the-letter-at-lunchtime.'

I ran home at the end of morning school. Mum produced a soggy unreadable mess from the washing machine. The letter had been in my football kit. I ran back to school and missed lunch.

When I got to the classroom I was so miserable my feet wouldn't go to the desk at the back. I looked round the class. Something had changed. At first I couldn't see what it was. Then I saw that some of the boys were talking to girls. Tom was talking to Marie Richards. Rich was talking to Karen Hardy.

It felt like when they used to do what I said, but this time I hadn't said anything. They were copying me and Abby. Perhaps everything would be all right. I hadn't used my fists. Perhaps I wouldn't have to use them any more, much.

The talking stopped. Everyone looked up to see what I would do. For a moment, I thought about giving them all a dose of ugly-vision. The moment passed, and I decided to let them live. I went to where Abby was sitting.

'All right,' I said. 'I'll try. As long as nobody starts anything.'

She smiled and the sun shone again. I sat down beside her.

'But I'm no Prince Charming,' I said.

'Who'd want a boring old prince when they could have a lovely frog like you?' she said.

Then she leaned over and kissed me on the cheek. Everybody cheered.

Wow!

baggy shorts

ALAN MACDONALD

'**A**nd there it is, the final whistle and Ditchley Rovers are through to a Wembley cup final for the first time in their history. The players are dancing around and hugging each other. The crowd (four parents and a kid in a pushchair) is going wild. Joss Porter, Ditchley's goal hero, runs towards the touch line with both arms in the air and salutes his dad. These are amazing scenes!'

I do commentaries like that in my head all the time – at school, on the bus, even underwater in the bath. But this commentary I was doing last Saturday afternoon was different. It was the real thing, I didn't have to make it up. Ditchley Rovers really had just made it through to our first ever Wembley final. And I scored one of the goals. Okay, so the ball bounced in off my knee but that's how I sent their goalkeeper the wrong way. And okay, so the final wasn't at Wembley Stadium, it was at Wembley Park. They're very similar, except the pitch at Wembley Park has hardly any grass and dips in the middle like a banana.

But that didn't matter to me. As I said to our manager the next day, 'We're in the final, that's all that counts.'

'Don't keep saying that, Joss,' said Dad. 'I'm trying to find Stanley Matthews.'

Dad was busy with his cigarette card collection. He's got boxes full of them. Cards he collected when he was a boy with colour pictures of ships, trains and wild birds. The ones I like best are his football cards. Famous players of the past with centre partings and teethy smiles.

Dad found the card he was looking for and held it up to show me.

'Stanley Matthews. The wizard of dribble. Now there was a real footballer. You never saw *him* kissing one of his team mates when he scored a goal.'

I nodded, but I wasn't really listening. All I could think about was Saturday and Ditchley Rovers v Top Valley. It was Top Valley's third cup final in a row. Really there ought to be a rule against teams hogging the cup. It was well known Top Valley creamed off all the best players in the area. Their manager went round all the school matches scouting for new talent. Most of Ditchley Rovers couldn't even get in their school team (me included). But Dad said that wasn't the point – everyone deserves a chance. It's not the winning that counts, it's the taking part. Which was another way of saying Top Valley were going to thrash us 8–0 on Saturday.

'I think it'll be a close game,' I said to Dad.

He didn't answer. Too busy glueing Stanley Matthews into his album.

'I mean the cup final, Dad. We'll probably only win by one goal.'

'It doesn't matter whether you win, Joss, as long as you all play your best.'

'You think we'll lose then? Our own manager doesn't give us a chance.'

'I didn't say that.'

'They're going to bury us, aren't they, Dad?'

Dad sighed heavily. 'Can't you just stop thinking about Saturday for five minutes?'

But I couldn't stop thinking about it. It was the cup final. Ditchley Rovers had never played in a final before and we weren't likely to play in one again. The truth was we were dead lucky to be in the final. There was a flu bug going round and two of the teams we were supposed to play against had to pull out because they couldn't raise a side. In the semi-final our goalie, Flip, made a string of blinding saves and then I scored a late winner with my knee. Dad said that if Eric Cantona had been playing against us that day he probably would have tripped over and sprained his ankle during the warm-up.

The trouble was, now that we were in the cup final I couldn't help it. At school, on the bus, under water in the bath … I was working on a new commentary.

'And it's all over. Top Valley hang their heads. They can't believe it. Ditchley Rovers – who nobody gave a chance going into this game – have made an amazing comeback. Three goals in three minutes from deadly Joss Porter have turned the game on its head. And now he's

being carried shoulder high by the Ditchley team as he lifts the cup to the crowd. The roar is deafening …'

It was all a dream, of course. Top Valley were going to slaughter us.

On Thursday we met for a practice session over at Wembley Park. Dad called us together for a team talk. He was wearing his navy tracksuit with the England 1966 badge on the pocket.

'Now we all know that Saturday is a big game for us. Our Joss has been going to bed with his kit on every night – just to make sure he doesn't miss the kick-off.'

Everyone looked in my direction and laughed. I hated it when Dad made stupid jokes about me. Sometimes I wished he wasn't our manager.

Dad went on. 'A cup final is special. There are plenty of kids who'd like to be in your boots on Saturday. But they're not. It's your chance, so make the most of it.'

I looked around. Matt, Flip, Sammy, Nasser and the rest were nodding their heads seriously. You could see they were as keyed up as I was.

We lined up for shooting practice against Flip.

'Flip me Joss! Why don't you break me fingers or something?' he said as he stopped my shot.

The truth is Flip's not a bad goalie. If it wasn't for him we'd never have reached the final. He's not very big but he isn't afraid of anything. This evening he was in great form, flinging himself down to stop a shot and springing up again like a jack-in-the-box. Hardly anything got past him.

A cold wind blows across Wembley Park on a winter evening. A thin mist drifted over from the river. It was Nasser who noticed the tall kid behind the goal watching us.

'Hey, Joss,' he grinned. 'You seen old baggy shorts over there? Think he wants a game?'

I looked behind the goal. The tall kid was standing to one side of the posts with a ball tucked under his arm. He had a body like a runner bean. Somehow it held up a pair of shorts that came down to his knees and flapped in the wind. He wore a green roll-neck jumper. Above it his big ears stuck out like mug handles under a flat grey cap. The total effect was like a jumble sale on legs.

By now Sammy, Matt, Nasser and the others had noticed him. They started making sniggering comments.

'Clock the gear, eh?'

'Is that Arsenal's away strip?'

'No, must be Oxfam's.'

'Let's sign him on. He can be our secret weapon.'

'Yeah, he can hide the match ball in his shorts.'

Nasser said the last joke too loud because Baggy Shorts frowned and looked at the mud.

'Shut up!' I said. 'He'll hear you.'

A few minutes later I went to get a ball from behind

the goal. Baggy Shorts was still standing there with the ball under his arm. The cold didn't seem to bother him. I wondered why he kept watching us.

'Hello,' I said. 'You from round here?'

He touched his cap and nodded seriously. 'Used to be.'

'What happened? Did you move away?'

'Kind of.' There was a pause. 'I'm a goalie,' he said, looking straight at me.

'Are you?'

'Yes. I'm a good goalie.'

'I bet you are. But we've already got a goalie. Flip. He's over there.'

I jerked my head in the direction of the goal. Baggy Shorts nodded again. 'I'm a good goalie,' he repeated, bouncing the ball and catching it in his big pale hands. I noticed it was made of heavy brown leather held together with a lace.

'We're playing here Saturday in the cup final,' I said. 'You can come and watch if you want.'

Baggy Shorts nodded again. 'I never played in a final. Never.' He looked away into the distance as if there was something just out of sight. The mist had got thicker. I realised I was shivering.

'Well, kick-off's at three.' I said. 'Come and support us. I gotta go now. See you.'

I ran back to the others. The shooting practice had stopped. Everyone was gathered round Flip who was sitting on the ground. Dad was kneeling beside him, looking at his nose which was an ugly swollen red.

'Ah flip me! Don't touch it!' he cried out.

'What happened?' I asked.

'I didn't know he was coming for the cross,' said Sammy. 'I was jumping to head the ball and Flip came out and somehow … I headed him instead.'

'It was my flippin' ball,' moaned Flip. 'I called for it.'

'Will he be all right?' I asked Dad. 'For Saturday, I mean? He will be able to play on Saturday, won't he?'

Dad helped Flip to his feet. 'It's probably just a nasty bruise. But I'll take him to the hospital to get it looked at just in case. The rest of you better go home. It's getting late.'

We trooped miserably off the field.

'Nice one Sammy,' I said. 'If Flip can't play on Saturday there goes our only chance. Without him Top Valley will murder us.'

As we were leaving I remembered Baggy Shorts again. I turned back to wave goodbye. But he'd gone, melted away into the mist.

It was Cup Final day, and we were sitting in the dressing room in silence, all staring at the floor. Dad had just asked if anyone wanted to play in goal. The news about Flip was bad. The hospital said his nose might be broken; it was hard to tell until the swelling went down. Broken or not, there was no way he could play in a cup final.

We'd have to play our sub, Gormless Gordon, at right back. That meant someone else had to go in goal.

The news was greeted in the dressing room as if someone had died. There was no point in kidding ourselves any longer. We'd lost the final before the game started. I could hear the commentary running through my head:

'And it's another one! This time through the goalkeeper's legs. This is turning into a massacre: 32–0 to Top Valley and there's still half an hour to go! Ditchley Rovers must wish the final whistle would blow and put them out of their misery.'

That's why no one was volunteering to put on the green jersey. The goalkeeper always gets the blame. He's the one the rest of the team picks on when they're losing badly. That's why I couldn't believe it when Dad spoke to me.

'Joss, you've played in goal before.'

I looked up in horror. 'That was only messing around in the park. I've never played in a proper match.'

'There's always a first time. You could do it.'

'Dad! No way! I'm a striker. I'd be hopeless in goal.'

'Well, somebody's got to. Listen all of you, Flip isn't coming. We've just got to put out the best team we can. And if we lose it's no disgrace. Now I'll ask again – is anyone willing to go in goal?'

I looked around at the rest of the team. Pleading with them: *'Not me, anyone but me, somebody else do it, please.'* No one would look at me. They stared at the floorboards as if they wanted to crawl underneath.

'Right, that's it then. Joss, you're in goal first half,' said Dad, losing patience. I picked up the green jersey he threw at me. It wasn't fair. He shouldn't be manager if he was going to pick on me.

Top Valley were already out on the pitch in their smart new kit. Red and white striped shirts with their names on the back. Just like professionals.

'Come on, you Valley kings! You'll murder this lot!' shouted their manager from the touch line. Most of their team were bigger than us. I recognised Gary Spencer who is top scorer for our school team. He gave me a nod.

'Hi Joss! They're not playing you in goal, are they?' I nodded miserably.

'You *must* be desperate,' he said, rubbing his hands together. You could see him imagining all the goals he was going to score.

The game kicked off. Top Valley sent the ball straight down the wing. We didn't clear it. A high ball came over. I started to come out for it, then changed my mind. As I tried to get back, the ball thumped into the corner of the net. Gary Spencer wheeled away with his arms going like windmills.

'Goooooooooal!'

Nasser shook his head at me in disbelief. 'Why didn't you come out?'

'Why didn't you mark him if you're so great?' I snapped back.

The rest of the first half we defended grimly, hardly ever getting past the halfway line. Top Valley went two up after twenty minutes. After that, I made a few lucky saves and we kept the score down by keeping ten players back and booting the ball anywhere.

As the minutes ticked toward half-time, I noticed the mist drifting in again from the river. I heard a ball bounce behind me and there was Baggy Shorts. He was wearing the same as before – grey cap, green jumper, huge baggy white shorts.

'Hi,' I said. 'Come to watch us get beaten?'

He stood to one side of my goal.

'Where's your goalie?' he asked.

'Broke his nose. Couldn't come. That's why they stuck me in goal.'

He nodded thoughtfully. 'I'm a goalie,' he said.

'Yeah,' I replied, 'you told me that the other day.'

'I'm good.'

'But you don't play for our team.'

'I could do, though.'

Baggy Shorts took off his flat cap and held it in both hands. His hair was cut short over his big ears and parted in the middle. He looked at me, his eyes full of longing.

'Please. I never played in a final. Never. Give me a chance.'

It came out in a rush. Then he put his cap back on and waited.

At that moment the referee blew for half time.

'You must be bonkers, Joss,' said Sammy. 'Look at him. He turns up out of nowhere in his grandma's bloomers and you want to play him in goal.'

'But we haven't got a goalkeeper,' I argued. 'We're going to get beaten anyway. What have we got to lose?'

'Another ten goals,' said Nasser.

I pulled off the green jersey.

'Well, who's going in goal for the second half then? I've done my bit.'

Nobody took the jersey from me. We all looked at Dad. It was his decision. He stared across at Baggy Shorts who stood a little way off, bouncing his old leather ball.

'Everyone deserves their chance,' said Dad.

Gormless Gordon went off and Baggy Shorts came on as a sub. I could see the Top Valley players grinning as Baggy Shorts took the field. He ran past them, shorts flapping in the wind and cap pulled down over his eyes.

Gary Spencer sidled up to me as we lined up for kick-off.

'Where'd you get him then? On special offer at Tesco's?'

I stared back at him coldly. I'd had enough of being the joke team. If we were going to lose then the least we could do was make a fight of it.

From the kick-off, Sammy passed to me and I burst through the middle. Top Valley were caught half asleep and my pass found Nasser in the penalty area. He shot first time, low into the corner: 2–1.

It was the start we needed to get back in the game. But it also stung Top Valley awake. They soon had the ball back up our end and Gary Spencer carved his way through our defence. He left three players on the ground as he raced into the penalty area.

There was only Baggy Shorts left between him and the goal. Spencer looked up to pick his spot. It was too easy. But in that second, Baggy Shorts came racing off his line like a greyhound and threw himself on the ball. Spencer couldn't take it in. One minute he had the ball, the next Baggy Shorts had whipped it off his boot and kicked it upfield. The small crowd watching clapped. Ditchley Rovers looked at each other in astonishment. Baggy Shorts wasn't just good, he was brilliant.

The rest of the game Top Valley tried to find a way to beat our new goalkeeper. They aimed for the corners. They rained in shots like cannonballs. They tried to dribble round him. But Baggy Shorts was a mind-reader. He seemed to know exactly where the ball was going. He leapt like a cat and pulled it out of the air. He rolled over, sprang to his feet, bounced the ball twice and sent it into orbit. With just ten minutes to go we got a goal back to level the scores at 2–2. Then, as the minutes ticked away, the disaster happened. Gary Spencer went through again, and again Baggy Shorts dived at his feet. But this time Spencer was waiting for it. He went sprawling over the goalkeeper and lay in the mud holding his leg.

'Ahh, ref! Penalty!'

Anyone could see it was an obvious dive but the referee blew his whistle and pointed to the spot.

Spencer made a miraculous recovery to take the penalty himself. He winked at Baggy Shorts with a smug grin on his face. Baggy Shorts didn't say a word, he went back on his goal-line. I walked away to the halfway line feeling sick. Three minutes to go and we were going to lose to the worst penalty ever given. But as Spencer placed the ball I couldn't help myself. I always do the commentary for penalties.

'And the crowd are hushed. Baggy Shorts crouches on his line. Spencer takes a run-up. He hits it hard, low, into the corner … it's … No! Baggy Shorts has saved it one-handed. An incredible save! Spencer has his head in his hands. Baggy Shorts gathers the ball. Sends a long kick upfield. Towards … ME! Help! Where is everybody?'

I just kept running towards the goal waiting for someone to tackle me. But nobody did. And as their goalkeeper came out I slipped the ball under his body. It rolled gently over the line. Goal – and this time I hadn't used my knee either.

The whistle went soon after. Ditchley Rovers had won the cup: 3–2 with a dramatic late winner from deadly Joss Porter. Just as I'd predicted all along. I was mobbed by the whole team, jumping on top of me until we were all rolling around in the mud, laughing. Dad was going round banging everybody on the back. I don't think he could quite believe it.

Then we had to line up for the cup to be presented. Sammy said, 'Where's Baggy Shorts? He should go up first. He was man of the match.'

We looked around. But we couldn't find him. No one knew where he'd gone. I looked back to the goalmouth where he'd saved the penalty, but there was no one there, only a fine mist drifting in from the river.

A few days after the cup final, Dad was working on his cigarette card collection again. I saw him stop with the glue in one hand and a card in the other. He was staring at something.

'What is it?' I asked. He handed me the card in his hand. It was from the football series. On the back it said:

Player number 132: Billy Mackworth. Goalkeeper.

Despite his boyish looks, Mackworth was a talented goalkeeper for Spurs. He should have been the youngest player to play at Wembley in the 1947 cup final. Sadly he died in a road accident a few days before the game. He never played in a cup final.

There was no mistaking the picture. He looked older but the two big ears still stuck out like mug handles under his cap. The eyes stared gravely into the distance. It was Baggy Shorts.

second half

One day those who make football will have to understand that there is no salvation without the artist. Of course you have to win, but you also have to admit defeat so that football can again be a source of emotion.

Eric Cantona

When you start strolling about it's hard to step up the tempo.

Alan Hansen of Liverpool and Scotland

You have to play to your strengths and my strength is my strength.

Stuart Pearce of Nottingham Forest, Newcastle United and England

Special

ALAN GIBBONS

'**M**rs Donnelly says I'm special,' said Roy. Only the way he said it told his mother special was a dirty word.

'That's good, isn't it?' she asked. But her voice had that little nervous shake that said she knew exactly what he was getting at.

'So how come I'm only special when I get taken out to read?'

At eleven o'clock every weekday morning Roy hated being special. Just hated it. That was when he had to collect his reading folder and sit at a table in the corridor with Mr Roberts. That was when he had to labour over the baby books they gave him, chewing over every word in the divvy stories about pigs that could talk and ducks that wore dresses. And what ten-year-old wants to read stuff like that?

'Sound it out,' Mr Roberts would say when Roy got stuck. And he got stuck a lot.

Sound it out yourself, Roy would think. Who cared if it was Percy or Penny Pig who wanted to cross the bumpety bridge? He would gladly have laid the dynamite that would have blown that stupid bumpety bridge to smithereens.

'You know what special means?' Roy asked. 'Thick, that's what. Everybody stares at me when I'm in the corridor.'

'Well, you're special to me,' said Mum, wincing visibly at the word *thick*. 'Now get out there and prove it.'

Roy glanced at his team-mates jogging on to the pitch. He'd prove it, all right. Footy was something he was good at, always had been. In fact, it was his ability with the ball that saved him from the skitting some of the other kids in Mr Roberts' group got.

'You ready, Roy?' Marty Collins called. Marty was the skipper of Gilmoss Rovers.

'Coming.'

'Play a blinder, son,' said Mum.

He did too, tackling hard in defence and making some strong forward runs through the opposition defence. He might be a wing back and supposedly a member of the Rovers' back four, but he was their second highest scorer. He felt great. Strong, quick, *special*.

His chance to be really special came when Marty knocked an early ball across. Roy came in like a train, but he was ever so slightly behind the play. Throwing himself at the ball, he could only meet it with a glancing header. As the ball flew high over the bar, there were howls of derision from the opposition, and groans from his own side.

'Wasted that one, didn't you Woy?' said Marty. He said it as a joke, but Roy recognized the prickly, impatient tone of his voice. He thought Roy should have got to it. Roy could only glare at his captain and fume. *Woy*! It was a nickname that came back to haunt him every time he messed up. Woy of the Wovers. All because of the stupid lisp he used to have when he was in the infants. Nobody would ever let him forget it, especially the time when he went up to the teacher and told her: 'I wuv you.' It was really unfair. Why did Marty have to skit him over it all the time? They were supposed to be mates, weren't they? And you don't skit mates. But Roy stood out. He was the sort of mate you just had to tease. He was a special mate.

Marty must have seen the hurt look on Roy's face, because he immediately chipped in with another comment. 'Better luck next time, eh?'

Roy gave him a grateful smile. 'Yes, better luck next time.'

Next time wasn't long coming. Billy Mac connected with a long clearance downfield and took it route one into the opposition goalmouth. A cool lay-off and he'd put Roy clear. Just a tap-in really: 1–0. Mum was cheering on the touch-line and giving him the thumbs up.

Roy was really motoring after that. A goal just before half-time and his hat-trick completed just after. There were goals by Billy Mac and Marty in between, giving the Rovers a 5–0 win.

'That was great,' said Mum as they got in the car. 'You should feel proud of yourself. You are special.'

Then the car radio started to play. *Three lions.* Not the best song in the world, but it still made him smile. Music always helped.

He gave Mum a smile. 'Special eh? Yes, maybe.'

Monday morning, eleven o'clock and he was back out in the corridor with Mr Roberts. Failing. Roy chewed over the memory of Sunday's 5–0 victory like old chewing gum, but the flavour had faded already. He might be a winner on the football field but here in school he was the world's number one loser. While Mr Roberts sorted the various sheets he carried about in his battered briefcase, Roy inspected his new book: *Cassie Cat goes to Sea.*

'Ready then, young man?' said Mr Roberts breezily, clicking his ballpoint pen.

'Yes, whatever,' grunted Roy. He hadn't even turned the cover, yet he hated Cassie Cat. Hated her with a vengeance.

'Good.' Mr Roberts was going to ignore Roy's surly answer. 'Read me the title.'

Roy had worked it out. *Cassie* had stumped him at first. It was a hard word, but weren't they all? Roy hated words, hated them because they scared him. If reading was as important as everybody said, why did it have to be so rotten hard?

'Something cat goes to sea,' he said.

'And what's the something?'

'Dunno.'

'Then try sounding it out. You know *c-a-*, don't you?'

'Yeah, ca.'

'Add an *s* sound.'

'Cass.'

'Now *-ie*. Remember, we've done this. It's like a *y* at the end of the word.'

'Cassie.'

Mr Roberts beamed. Roy didn't return the smile. You think you've taught me something, he thought. Well, you never, because I knew it already.

'Good lad,' said Mr Roberts. 'Read on.'

It had been a slow start, and it got worse. Roy toiled over nearly every word. Soon his neck was burning with shame and embarrassment, and every time Mr Roberts tried to help, it just made things worse. Reading was hard and nothing anybody did was going to make it any easier.

Roy's suffering was finally brought to an end when Mr Roberts glanced at his watch. 'Oh well, time's up, Roy. I've got to fit Jennifer in before lunch.'

Roy slipped gratefully into class and dropped into his seat next to Marty. Whenever Roy went out with Mr Roberts, Marty had to brief him on what the class had been doing. That's why his teacher Mrs Fay didn't mind them talking.

'Heard who we've got in the first round of the Cup?' asked Marty.

'No, who?'

'Only Clubmoor Colts.'

'But we play them this Sunday in the league.'

'That's what I'm telling you. We're playing them twice in a fortnight, first in the league, then in the Cup.'

'Bit of a coincidence, isn't it?'

Marty shrugged his shoulders. 'It happens.'

Roy was about to say something else when Mrs Fay looked across at them.

'Marty Collins,' she said. 'Are you quite sure you're discussing the Spartan army?'

Roy stared down at his worksheet. There was a picture of a half-naked bloke with a funny hat and a sword.

'The what?'

'Spartans,' Marty said loudly for Mrs Fay's benefit. 'Bunch of Greek fellers. Rock hard.'

Roy was interested, but only for a few moments. When he couldn't make head nor tail of the library book Marty passed him, he copied a couple of sentences off him and stared out of the window. Reading was hard. As in impossible.

Devastated. That was the only word for Roy's mood the following Sunday morning at final whistle. Clubmoor hadn't just beaten Rovers: they'd taken them to the cleaners. What hurt was that they'd done it by completely dominating the Rovers down the right flank, and that was Roy's patch. There was this kid playing for Clubmoor, Kieran McCann, and he'd had the beating of Roy right from the kick-off. McCann had come off the blocks like he meant to prove something. He did too. He proved that Roy wasn't so special on the pitch, after all. As he sat on the touch-line, arms hugging his knees, head sagging, he relived every minute of their one-sided duel.

It started badly when McCann turned him inside-out in the first minute, going round the outside to whip in the cross that lead to Clubmoor's opening goal. Then it got worse. A lot worse. Three of Clubmoor's first-half goals came from right-sided crosses, and that was down to Roy's inability to stop McCann. The Rovers rallied a bit in the second half and their better form took some of the pressure off Roy. It didn't prevent one last act of humiliation, though. In the last minute Clubmoor were leading 7–2 and McCann picked the ball up on the half-way line. The moment he started his run, Roy was backing off. He had a lump in his throat. He was going to get taken again, and everybody was watching.

'Get into him, Roy,' yelled Marty.

But Roy's bottle had gone. He backed off and backed off and that's when it happened. Right in front of goal he slipped and fell. Smack on his backside. McCann gave a triumphant grin and ran on to slot home his side's eighth goal.

'Well, you certainly got into him,' said Marty. '*Woy*!'

With that, the skipper had stormed off. Roy felt the bitter taste of defeat in his mouth. Sure, they'd lost before, but never this heavily. For the first time he had to come to terms with a cruel truth. Even on the pitch there were kids who could play better. Loads of them. Even there he wasn't special.

It was nearly a week before Roy started to get over it. Saturday night to be exact, the eve of their re-match with Clubmoor. Music helped. As usual. And it was a football anthem that did it. As usual. Roy sat in his room brooding over the 8–2 thrashing and listening to the radio. That's when it came on. *You'll Never Walk Alone*. He heard the piano playing a rhythm like falling rain and the singer's voice, sad and soft like the wind off the Mersey, driving out the words that had hoisted a million football scarves.

That's right, that's what he'd do: walk on, fight on. There was always another day.

Roy started to smile. He wouldn't be afraid of the dark, he wouldn't be afraid of anything. Who did this McCann lad think he was anyway? He was only another snotty-nosed kid from the North End. It's not like he was Robbie Fowler or Steve McManaman or something. He'd had a good day. Maybe on Sunday it would be Roy's turn to shine.

Too right! And this time there was going to be a golden sky, his golden sky. His! Suddenly Roy was laughing as if all eight goals they'd let in had been flukes.

'You sound happy,' said Mum poking her head round the door.

'Yes,' said Roy as the song's last drumbeat died away. 'That's because I am.'

The strain on Roy's face must have been showing because Marty came up to him at half-time.

'Everything all right?' he asked.

'Yes, why shouldn't it be?'

Roy's reply was a fierce challenge. He'd kept McCann at bay, hadn't he? It hadn't been easy, either. Roy knew the leggy Clubmoor player had the beating of him if he wasn't on his game. But he'd kept at it, bumping, pushing, crowding, never giving his opponent an inch. He'd stuck to his man like a limpet.

'I was only asking,' said Marty, taken aback. 'You've been sound.'

'Yes,' said Roy flatly. He wasn't taking any flannel off Marty. One slip and he'd be getting the *Woy* treatment again. 'I know.'

He was better than all right in the second half. His marking had demoralised McCann and he was able to make a few forward runs of his own. They didn't come to anything though, and the teams were stalemated at 0–0.

'Something's got to give,' said Marty. 'I can't take the tension.'

'Something *did* give. It was Marty. He was trying to work the ball out of defence when he gave the ball away. To McCann of all people! The Clubmoor winger had been fading, but suddenly he saw his chance to be a hero. A moment after intercepting Marty's sloppy ball, he was bearing down on Roy. Go past him and he would have the goal at his mercy.

'Get into him!' came the cries of Roy's team-mates.

Roy's heart was crawling into his mouth. All the time McCann was driving forward they were staring at each other. This was the final showdown. Roy watched the jinking run and he was afraid. Scared witless of McCann's pace. He held off and held off, expecting McCann to make his break. When it came, the drive into the box was unstoppable. McCann pushed the ball and flashed past.

'No-o-o,' came the voices of his team mates.

The Rovers might have given up, but not Roy. McCann was past him and into the penalty area. Roy's tackle had to be inch-perfect. Turning, he steadied himself. He remembered the strains of

You'll Never Walk Alone. This time, it wasn't on the radio. It was in his head.

He didn't give up. He hoped. He dared. Keeping his eye on the ball, he propelled himself forward.

He slid across the greasy turf. The ball had sat up for McCann and Roy made contact. For a second he winced. Touch the man and it was a penalty. But his boot met the ball. Clean as a whistle. Then Chris, their goalie was in attendance. Grinning gratefully at Roy, he dribbled it out of harm's way. In an instant Roy was running forward to give Chris a target.

'Mine!' he bawled.

Chris wasn't about to refuse him. Gathering the ball on the edge of the area, Roy powered forward. He was on fire. Beating two opponents by sheer pace, he had carved an opening for himself.

'Roy,' yelled Marty, peeling away to the left. 'First time ball.'

Roy released it and Marty did the business with the crisp, square pass. They'd done it. One–nil. The moment the whistle went, Roy was mobbed. Up against a far better player he'd stuck to his guns and come through. He was so high he started to do something he'd only ever done in the privacy of his own room. He actually started to sing. *You'll Never Walk Alone*. That's when he noticed everyone staring. Like he was doing something special.

Just how special he found out a couple of weeks later. It was their class assembly and Mr Roberts had got him to sing. For the whole school! He felt a divvy at first. For a start, Mum was in the front row. And that's not all. Some of the kids were pointing, others were laughing. But the moment Roy started to sing, the entire hall fell silent. Three hundred kids and not a murmur. And at the end there was this long silence, then applause. Loads of it. Like heavy rain.

'That was amazing,' said Marty afterwards. 'Mr Roberts says you've got a gift.'

'It's not so special,' said Roy. 'It's easy.'

Funnily enough, Roy was saying the same thing to Mr Roberts at eleven o'clock that morning. This time he wasn't talking about singing. He meant his book.

'So what's the cat called?' asked Mr Roberts.

'Cassie,' Roy answered. 'Stupid name for a cat.'

'I agree,' said Mr Roberts. 'We'll try reading some football magazines next week.'

'I'd like that,' said Roy. 'Reading's easy.'

It wasn't, but somehow it was never quite so difficult again.

The Secret Weapon

SAM JACKSON

It's 7–6!'

'More like 6 all!'

'Look.' Simon put his hands on his waist and glared at Joanne. 'I'm the one keeping score. We had a penalty, remember?'

Jo flashed him an impish smile.

'Which you *missed*, Si!' She ran a hand through her short black hair and peered at Simon with dark eyes.

'Oh … errr,' Simon shrugged as the rest of the lunch-time football crew gathered around. 'But we had another one!' he said excitedly. 'I blasted it past Ryan!'

Jo recalled Simon's stocky frame belting the ball towards goal. Ryan had stood still in the goal, like a Subbuteo figure with his arms poised for a catch. He had stayed still as the ball whisked past his ear, not moving until it had bounced off the mesh fence and walloped him on the back of the head.

Short and cheeky, Ryan was Joanne's best friend, the first year's classroom entertainer. His antics usually had everyone cracking up at least once during the frantic lunch-hour game up on the tennis courts.

'Well, I think we all remember that one,' Jo said

with a chuckle. She gave Ryan a quick dig in the ribs. 'But it's still 6 all, Si.'

Jo sighed. It was the same every lunch-time. About five minutes before the afternoon bell was due to ring out across the courts and playing fields, Simon would become anxious that his team wasn't winning and would try to make out they were one or two up. Jo and Ryan were used to it, but they wished that Simon could just coolly lose the odd game without getting into such a flap. Since he'd been made captain of the first year Sandycliffe High team, he'd become fiercely competitive.

Arguing with Simon was pretty pointless. Jo and Ryan liked to wind him up if they could. His pale blue eyes would grow wide and serious and his shock of ginger hair trembled as he tried to get his point across. Ryan squatted down and began imitating the actions of a large flapping bird about to take off.

Simon ignored him. 'Ask Matt,' he yelled.

Matt Dean was over by the steps on what Jo thought must be his eightieth keep-up, in a world of his own with his precious Adidas ball. Gorgeous Matt Dean, tall and blue-eyed, was Sandycliffe's top goalscorer and master skillsman.

'Hey! David Beckham!' Ryan yelled to him. 'What's the score?'

Matt glanced distractedly towards the group. 'Six all.'

Simon threw Matt a murderous look as the others burst out laughing.

'Let's show him,' Ryan said to Jo before jogging off towards his goal.

They started again from the centre. The lunch-time games on the courts were always frantic and Jo's legs were never free of colourful bruises. Simon was good at dishing them out, the way he blundered in at anyone who had possession. But this time Jo nudged the ball left as Simon came thundering towards her. Suddenly Ryan came streaking into the attacking third. Jo touched the ball into his path as he powered through the defence and fired a shot through the middle of the bag markers.

He threw his arms up in an exaggerated celebration. 'Peter Schmeichel eat your heart out! Seven–six to us!'

'Nice one!' Jo told him as they headed in for afternoon lessons.

'Great pass from our lunch-time guest star!' Ryan said, in the style of John Motson. 'If I were Captain I'd let you in the school team. You'd easily make it if we picked the best eleven. Simon's such a wally not letting you in. Mr Shaw shouldn't leave it up to him anyway.'

Ryan grinned cheekily. 'You could play up front with Matt,' he said with a wink and proceeded to break into song. 'Because heeeeee's gorgeous!'

Jo shoved him away playfully.

'I'm not bothered really,' she said. 'It's just knowing that Simon and some of the others won't have me in the real team ... It just makes me more determined. Just one chance is all I want.'

'Mr Shaw said they're mad not to have you,' Ryan said.

Jo stared at him. 'No kidding!'

Simon jogged up alongside them. 'Matt said he made a mistake earlier with the scores so I guess your effort made it seven all.'

Ryan looked at Jo and shook his head. He placed a sympathetic arm around Simon's shoulders and spoke in his ear in low, soothing tones. 'Si, it really is okay to lose the lunch-time game. You're not going to get suspended or anything.'

Simon tutted and walked off towards the science labs.

Jo glanced up at the main block and saw Mr Chambers glaring down at them from the first floor maths room, where she and Ryan were due two minutes ago.

'Oh-oh,' said Ryan. The two of them sprinted to the double doors.

Jo sat in her usual place, next to Nikki at the back of the classroom. Bubbly Nikki Grainger was in trouble almost every lesson for talking and giggling. With Ryan on her other side, Jo wondered whether she should perhaps move if she was to have any hope of getting a half decent maths report this year.

It was difficult trying to concentrate on Mr Chambers, standing by the blackboard barking algebra examples, with Nikki whispering ridiculous questions about Matt Dean every ten seconds.

When Mr Chambers began rummaging in his desk Jo turned to her. 'For the millionth time, Nikki. I play footie with the lads at lunch because I enjoy it, not because I want to be near Matt. Okay! If you like him so much, why don't you join us?'

'Oh, I couldn't,' Nikki said quickly, fiddling with a long strand of wavy blonde hair. 'I'd be useless.'

Ryan leaned across Jo. 'You're dead right there,' he said flatly.

Nikki lurched at Ryan with her ruler, hitting his hand with several loud slapping noises. Jo wasn't surprised to look up and discover that they had attracted the attention of the stern maths teacher.

Ryan spoke into Jo's ear while trying to wrestle the ruler from Nikki's determined grasp. 'I reckon you should turn up to our practice tomorrow.'

Jo shook her head.

'Okay then,' Ryan went on. 'Your netball practice is tonight, yeah?'

Jo turned to him sharply.

Ryan had time to grin and say, 'I'll see you there then,' before his name was bellowed from the front of the classroom.

'Nikki must hold the record for getting sent out of

Chambers' class!' Jo said to her friend Lucy as she finished fastening her red games skirt, 'And Ryan was ordered to sit on the front row with the boffins for the next fortnight.'

Lucy gathered her thick brown hair into a high bunch.

'Why *don't* you go to the practice like Ryan suggested?' she asked Jo. 'The others wouldn't mind.'

Jo sighed. 'I don't reckon they want to be seen to go against Simon, whatever his problem is. He'd really flip if he thought they were all against him.'

Miss Irving handed Jo a net full of orange netballs as the girls passed her on the way out of the P.E. corridor. 'Be with you in a minute, girls,' she said.

It was ten minutes later when Miss Irving strolled towards the courts, and Ryan was beside her, dressed in tracky bottoms and trainers.

'What on *earth* is he doing?' Lucy spluttered.

Jo eyed the approaching duo suspiciously. She pulled a face. 'I don't think I want to find out.'

'Right, girls!' said Miss Irving as the curious netball squad gathered round. 'We have a new recruit today. I'm not sure whether Ryan has any real intention of representing Sandycliffe at netball … But as you know, everyone is welcome to have a go. So, Ryan,' she turned to the surprise guest who was trying to hide an idiotic grin. 'Are you familiar with the rules of the game?'

Ryan smiled confidently. 'Not a clue, miss! But I'm eager to learn.'

'Fine!' Miss Irving looked at him with a slightly glazed expression. Jo felt herself cringing as a giggle rippled around the group. 'Lucy and Jo will fill you in.'

Jo dragged Ryan away from the group.

'You're off your trolley if you think this is going to make me go to footy practice,' she whispered to Ryan sternly.

Ryan shrugged, plainly enjoying the stir he was causing.

'Irving was cool about it,' he said cheerfully. 'I should have a laugh, looks easy enough. Like basketball, but duller, yeah?'

Lucy let out a wicked laugh. 'Just you wait,' she said.

Miss Irving handed Ryan the Goal Attack bib for the practice game, and with a glint in her eye promptly organised Deborah Burdett as the opposing Goal Defence to mark him. If there was one person, Jo thought, who *wouldn't* be amused at Ryan turning up it was Deborah – the Simon of the netball crew. Tall and hefty, Deborah towered over Ryan as they stood side by side, poised for the whistle.

From the outset Deborah stuck to Ryan like a giant limpet. Jo watched as his fixed grin slowly settled into an angry grimace as he battled with his marker. Lucy giggled throughout the action. Jo was loving it as well. Seeing her laugh-a-minute friend becoming more furious by the moment was a treat. When Ryan did manage to snatch a pass, Deborah arrived like a giant spider in front of him, waving her arms around to cover any direction he might pass the ball.

Ryan managed one shooting chance after twenty minutes. As he held the ball aloft, sizing up the shot, determination etched on his face, Deborah settled into her defensive stance, balancing on one leg and leaning in like a huge crane to place a broad palm two inches from the ball. Ryan teased her with a mischievous grin and moved the ball from side to side. As Deborah wobbled, Ryan hurled the ball. It crashed against the high fence five yards behind the ring to an outburst of hysterical laughter. It all ended abruptly when the cheeky pretender received a stiff elbow to the chin. Deborah did an expert job at making it look like an accident.

'I have to say,' Ryan said as they walked home, touching his jaw tenderly, 'that was one of the worst half hours of my life. Deborah Burdett is a nightmare. She's possessed!'

Lucy and Jo giggled.

'Like basketball but duller,' said Jo, mocking Ryan's earlier words.

'I'll be back!' he said dramatically.

'Hard luck about not making the team for the game against St Paul's,' Lucy teased.

Ryan turned to Jo.

'But the point is,' he said, sounding like a teacher, 'that if I *had* been good enough, I would have been picked. I made a total dork of myself to show you that you should forget about Simon and his "No Girls" rule and go for it!'

Jo looked at him. 'Thanks for making us all laugh, Ry, but we'll see.'

Thursday's lunch-hour game had been going a few seconds before Jo dodged past a defender to score. Ryan delivered a stinging congratulatory slap on the back. Lucy and Nikki were watching from the steps. Not the football, but Matt Dean. They clapped loudly when he sent a left-footed shot skidding across the concrete past Ryan.

Simon became stressed about the score at the usual time, but even *he* couldn't dream up four goals that didn't exist.

As they piled down the steps at the end of the lunch-hour, Lucy stood up, boldly blocking Simon's path.

'Si, how come you won't let Jo be in the team?' she asked coolly.

Simon smiled awkwardly. The gang gathered round and waited for his response. His cheeks flushed a deep red before he seemed to gather himself and slung his bag over his shoulder.

'Not good for our image,' he said flatly and walked away.

Nikki shouted after him. 'What *image*? We're useless!'

Simon didn't look round.

'He's got a mate who plays for St Paul's, Adam Bennett.' It was Matt who spoke.

Everyone leaned in closer, interested in this new revelation.

'Si said Bennett would never let him forget it if we had a girl playing for us.'

Apart from Lucy blurting her disgust, the news was received with a thoughtful silence.

Nikki gazed up at Matt. 'What do you think?'

Matt paused for a moment. 'I think Jo's good,' he said matter-of-factly. 'I wouldn't mind if I got more service up front.' He shrugged and suddenly, as if sensing the complete attention of the surrounding crowd, he strode away. Nikki almost fell flat on her face in a effort to gather up her bag and follow him.

'So. Simon's scared of looking like a wally in front of his little friend?' Ryan sneered.

'Bennett's totally rubbish!' Parmi said. 'He scored the worst own goal ever that time. He's the guy that always tries those stupid bicycle kicks.'

Ryan burst out laughing. 'No wonder he doesn't want us to get any better!'

Jo looked out across the fields as she headed for the school gates. Down on the bottom pitch the goals had been set out, ready for the evening football practice. Lucy's words during History still echoed around her head.

'The others want you,' Lucy had urged.

Jo sighed. It just wasn't her style to force her way into anything. Simon would have to ask her. Rounding the corner, Jo almost collided with the broad figure of Mr Shaw.

'Sorry, I was miles away,' Jo said apologetically.

'Joining us?' the teacher asked with a broad smile.

Jo shook her head.

'It'll be a tough one on Saturday against St Paul's. I'd love to show that games teacher of theirs we can do something.' Mr Shaw mused.

Jo sat in the shelter on Saturday morning and watched the double-decker bus sail past. Lucy was late again. Jo glanced at her watch. Half-eleven. Sandycliffe would be well into the second half of the game against St Paul's.

Jo looked up when she heard hurried footsteps. Expecting Lucy, she felt a shudder of surprise to see Matt jogging past. He spun round as she called his name. Matt looked stressed, yet he was clearly relieved to see Jo.

'Lifesaver!' he said breathlessly. 'Got to get my kit

up to school for Mr Shaw ... wants to send faulty shirts back after the game ...'

Jo frowned at him. 'But why aren't you playing?'

Matt swallowed and began to speak more regularly. 'My brother set fire to our living-room, the little pain, just as I was about to set off. Mum thought he was old enough to be left on his own as well. Our neighbour is sitting with him while I take this up to the school, but he's going out so I can't be long. Will you do me a massive favour and take my kit to Mr Shaw?'

Jo took the handle of the heavy black bag.

'They must be playing with ten men,' said Matt. 'Andy couldn't make it either, I just saw him.'

Jo watched him dash away. She looked at her watch again. If she hurried, she would get to Sandycliffe just as the match was ending. An idea was beginning to take shape.

Lucy appeared by the shelter, her hair wild from the wind.

'I've got to get to the school,' Jo said urgently and she began to run.

Five minutes later she was beside Mr Shaw on the touch-line.

'Matt's kit,' she explained. The P.E. teacher thanked her distractedly, not taking his eyes away from the game. He told Jo the score was 1–0 to St Paul's. The match was nearly over.

'Turning up to play St Paul's with ten men!' Mr

Shaw said angrily. 'Their man thinks we're a bunch of fools!'

Jo noticed the smug-looking rival coach.

The action was in the St Paul's penalty box. Jo glanced at Ryan, standing on the edge of his area. His hands in the huge keeper's gloves were frantically beckoning her. It was the last push Jo needed.

She threw away her heavy coat and began rummaging in Matt's bag. She pulled on the white number ten shirt over her plain top and the long, baggy shorts over black leggings. Her own suede trainers would have to do.

Mr Shaw hadn't noticed the frantic activity beside him. His eyes nearly popped out of his head when he turned and saw Jo ready to join the action. Without a word he signalled to the referee. Jo took a last glance around and saw Lucy thudding down the slope.

'Go for it!' she yelled and Jo ran on to the pitch feeling more nervous than she had ever felt in her whole life.

Of all the Sandycliffe team, Simon was the last to see Jo. A look of utter shock swept over his face as she sprinted towards the St Paul's area. Jo stood in front of him, waiting for instructions, but Simon just gawped. He glanced towards a fair-haired boy dressed in the dark red St Paul's strip. The boy was smiling slyly at Simon. Jo realised this must be Adam Bennett.

'Where do you want me?' Jo's shriek seemed to snap Simon out of his trance. 'We ... we've got a corner,' he stammered, then focused on Jo properly. 'You take it'.

Jo raced to the spot. Ryan had approached the half-way line. He was clapping his hands madly. 'Float one in,' he yelled.

Jo stood five paces back from the ball. 'Please don't let me hoof it behind the goal,' she whispered. As she took powerful strides into the shot, a sudden gust of wind lashed in towards the goal. The ball left Jo's foot with a full, powerful contact – too far behind the waiting Sandycliffe trio of Simon, Parmi and Dave – until it began to curl in towards the crowd in the box.

Jo stood frozen to the spot. Parmi and Simon rose together towards the floating cross. Sandycliffe's two tallest players drew in the St Paul's defence. But at the last moment, a reverse gust whipped the ball away from its intended target. It passed by the scrambling bunch of players who had launched themselves towards the cross. But suddenly Ryan was there streaking up to the far post to slide the ball past St Paul's sprawling goalkeeper.

Ryan led the charge towards Jo with his usual two-armed celebration and Simon was right behind him.

'Wicked cross!' Simon shrieked.

Ryan and Jo were carried along amid hysterical

whoops of delight from the rest of the team. Jo couldn't help noticing the mean stare Adam Bennett was giving Simon.

Ryan nudged him. 'Your mate looks mad,' he said.

But Simon didn't look bothered. 'No wonder,' he said, grinning broadly. 'He doesn't have a secret weapon, does he?'

The last minute went by in a complete whirl for Jo. She watched, dazed, as Bennett legged Simon over in the St Paul's area. The Sandycliffe captain blasted home the free shot to make it two-one to the home side. At the final whistle Mr Shaw looked almost delirious with delight. Lucy gave Jo a massive hug.

The Sandycliffe team walked away from the school still buzzing with excitement.

'Was one go enough, then?' Ryan asked Jo.

Jo looked round at them all. 'For now,' she said, unable to hide a huge grin. 'I can't take this kind of madness every Saturday!'

Top Striker

WILLIAM CROUCH

The new girl looked around at the supporters lining the pitch. Then she stared at the twenty-two players ready for the kick-off.

'This is weird, Rachel,' she said. 'Why don't they start? And where's the ball?'

'It's coming,' said Rachel. 'Listen!'

The sound was uncanny. Like a strong wind in a gale, thought Tasha. Or Mum's pressure cooker, or maybe someone letting air out of a giant-sized tyre.

Then she saw it. Behind the woods, on the other side of the field, was a huge blue blob. A massive hot-air balloon! The crew were hastily adding more gas to the tongue of flame in an effort to get over the trees.

'They've made it,' said Rachel. 'Now watch, Tasha.'

The balloon cleared the trees and dived low over the field. As it reached the pitch it seemed to hover. One of the crew leaned out of the basket and neatly dropped the ball into the centre circle.

'Wow!' said Tasha. 'You said Dale Valley Rovers had problems, Rache. Tell me about it. Do they do this every week?'

'Sort of,' said Rachel.

Tasha stared up as the balloon passed overhead.

She read the catch-phrase painted in huge white letters: 'Blinks Butter Biscuits are Best.'

The ref positioned the ball and whistled the match into play. Danny, a Dale Valley striker, pushed the ball forward. Kev came from midfield to take it while Danny raced into Cowley Cobblers' half. Then, to everyone's amazement, Dale Valley's second striker ran for the ball. He collided with Kev, and both fell to the ground, Kev clutching his ankle and roaring at the striker. The ball was taken by a Cobblers' winger who lobbed it across to give his strikers time to get to the Dale Valley goal area. A clever pass from a Cobblers' midfielder gave the ball to a striker who, with perfect footwork, ran through the defenders and banged the ball into the net. Rob, the Dale Valley keeper, didn't stand a chance. Score: 1–0 after less than a minute's play!

'See what I mean?' said Rachel. 'We're in big trouble.'

'Pathetic,' agree Tasha. 'Who is that dimwit?'

'His name's Sidney Blinks. His dad's a millionaire and chairman of the youth club. Money's no problem. We've got everything: new buildings, gym, games room, playing field. And we've got Sidney. His dad insists that he's a striker.'

The two girls were joined by a group of Dale Valley supporters. The expressions on the kids' faces – utter misery and frustration – portrayed their opinion of Sidney Blinks.

'What can we do with him?' shouted Julie Jones.

'He's got to go,' muttered Andy Hugget. 'We must get rid of him.'

'Agreed,' said Rachel, 'but if Sidney goes, so does the club.' She took Tasha's arm. 'This is Tasha,' she said. 'Her family have just moved into Dale Valley. She's dead keen on football so I'm telling her the problem. Three years ago, Tasha, Dale Valley kids had nothing, not even a patch to bounce a ball on. Then Mr Johnnie Blinks, the world famous biscuit manufacturer, moved into the Manor House. He built the club and showered us with goodies.'

'Only because of his dear little Sidney,' shouted Julie.

'We all know that,' said Rachel. 'Don't yell at me, Julie. We're in this together.'

She was interrupted by a roar from the crowd. One of the Cobblers' strikers was hopping around in sheer agony and the ref was awarding a free kick. Sidney had done it again.

The group moved along the touchline to be nearer the action. The ball seemed to be permanently in Dale Valley's half and in the net far too often.

The score was now 5–0. Rob was in despair. He muttered, 'Not my fault,' when he saw Terry Bond, the coach and team manager, coming towards him.

'Don't worry,' said Terry. 'It'll be better next week.'

'You said that last week,' sighed Rob. 'It just gets worse. Mark and Trev were the best defenders we ever had. And they've left because they can't stand Sidney Blinks any longer.'

Terry knew the problem.

'Why don't you have girls in the team?' Tasha asked Rachel. 'I'd play.'

'So would I,' said Rachel. 'But Mr Blinks won't hear of it. He doesn't like girls.'

'Anyway,' said Sam Walker, the youngest and smallest supporter of Dale Valley Rovers, 'girls can't play football. Yuk!'

'I'll take you on any day,' said Tasha. 'Look, why don't we get a ball and have a kickabout under the trees?'

'Great!' said Rachel. 'Five-a-side?'

They borrowed a ball from Terry and made a couple of goals with their coats.

Tasha drew her long dark hair up over her head and fixed it with a hairband. She took the ball and headed it against the trunk of a tree. She kept this going, counting as she did so; stopping when she got to six. Then she juggled it on her knees, trapped it, dribbled it around Sam and Andy, just to show that girls are tops, and lobbed it over to Rachel.

She was surprised when Rachel neatly trapped it and booted it back to her.

'You're good, Rachel,' she said.

'Yeah,' said Rachel. 'Got three brothers. All football crazy. But where did you learn those tricks, Tasha?'

'Dad's a striker. He's just transferred to the Wanderers.'

'You mean Bigley Wanderers?'

'Yeah.'

'Phew! He must be good.'

Other kids came to watch. This was real football. Rachel and Tasha picked sides: a keeper, three midfielders and a striker.

Tasha was great. She scored a hat-trick within the first few minutes of the game. But then Rachel took Julie Jones out of goal and put in Sam. He had one ambition: to play as keeper for Dale Valley Rovers. Today he almost qualified. They finished the game 6–4.

'Tell you what,' said Andy, 'let's kick out silly Sidney and make Tasha our top striker. We'd murder the lot of 'em.'

Nobody spoke as they took their coats and made for the pitch. Then Julie Jones said: 'I've got an idea.'

'If it's the same as Andy's you know what to do with it,' said Rachel.

'Okay,' sighed Julie. 'But I think we should have a secret meeting.'

'Secret meeting? Where? What for?'

'We could have it in your dad's big shed. And talk

about the team's problem. If we lose next week against Denby Flyers we might as well take up tiddlywinks or Junior Scrabble. It'll be nine defeats. One after the other.'

'Are you inviting Sidney and his dad?'

'Course not. Get real, Rache. We can't say what we like in the club because of Sidney. But if we have a secret meeting, someone may come up with an idea.'

Rachel considered this. Maybe Julie had a point. 'Okay. Ten o'clock tomorrow morning. I'll kick the word around.'

They were just in time to see Dale Valley's only goal. The game was still in the home team's half when Gary, in midfield, took the ball and fired it powerfully into the opposition's territory. Danny held it neatly, slipped past two defenders and slotted it home.

'Thirteen–one,' said Rachel. 'Could have been worse.'

'Yes,' agreed Tasha. 'So who's the striker? I'm impressed.'

The whole gang came to the meeting. The shed was massive; Rachel's dad had started his business there before moving to the industrial estate. Rachel banged on the table. 'Okay guys, let's get started. This is a proper meeting like we used to have before we got the club.'

'Before we got Sidney, you mean,' said Rob.

'Leave it out, Rob,' said Andy.

Rachel banged on the table again. 'Order!' she called. 'No more interruptions or I'll get Sam to throw you out.'

There was a guffaw but the gang settled down. There were plenty of seats. The shed was littered with empty wooden crates, a few broken chairs and a couple of ancient oak pews that had come from the church hall.

'This idea was Julie's,' said Rachel, 'so I'm going to ask her to begin the meeting. Over to you, Julie.'

'Well,' said Julie, 'we all moan about Sidney, but what do we do about it? Nothing.'

'What *can* we do?' said Rob.

'Shut up and listen!' snapped Julie. 'We've got to win next Saturday's match against the Flyers. We can do it if we haven't got Sidney and if Mark and Trev come back as defenders. Agreed?'

Most of the gang nodded.

'Mark, would you and Trev come back if we didn't play Sidney?' she asked.

'Yeah.'

'Good. Suggestions then on how to get rid of Sidney. Be serious.'

'Tie 'im up and put 'im in the river,' shouted Rob.

Julie was a first-class chairperson. She ignored Rob and went on. 'We've got to remember his dad always brings him to the match so we've got to take care of Mr Blinks as well.'

The gang came up with ideas. They were out of this world and quite impossible. Things like, tell him he's won the Lottery and will he go and collect the money on Saturday; Bigley wants him for their mascot but he must go to every match; Hollywood are making a film about kid's football and they want him to be the star.

They talked for over an hour and then Danny, who'd said nothing, put up his hand.

'Shush, you kids!' yelled Julie. 'Danny's got an idea. Over to you, Danny.'

'Okay,' said Danny. 'Sidney wants to make his name in football so let's put him on television.'

'How?'

'Saturday night's *Sports Quiz*. We get a message to Sidney and his dad just before the match starts saying that the Quiz want them to take part in that evening's show and will they come to the studio straight away for a rehearsal. They'll jump at it. By the time they find it's a hoax we'll have buried the Flyers. We'll have had Mark and Trev back as defenders and we'd have played a new striker.'

For a moment there was silence and then the gang began to hammer in the questions.

'Why wait until Saturday afternoon before giving them the invite?'

'Who's going to make the telephone call?'

'Who's the new striker?'

'Go on, Danny,' said Rachel. 'This is fantastic.'

'Okay,' said Danny. 'One at a time. If Mr Blinks gets a call before Saturday he's got plenty of time to find out it's a hoax. Agreed?'

There was a nodding of heads.

Danny went on. 'We'll get someone, perhaps Simon, Rachel's brother, to 'phone from the call box down the road. We'll give him a signal from the car park when they arrive.'

'Brilliant,' said Julie Jones. 'So who's our new striker, Danny?'

'She's sitting right here,' said Danny, putting his hand on Tasha's shoulder.

The next day Rachel and Julie went to see the club's coach. 'I hope it works,' Terry said, 'but don't count me in. When Mr Blinks finds out there'll be trouble and I don't want to lose my job.'

Simon was enthusiastic. 'Yeah. I'll make the call,' he said. 'I've never liked Johnnie Blinks or his sneaky little boy. I'll be at the call box and you can wave to me when he arrives. I'll chat him up and then invite him to the television studio.'

For the rest of the week they practised hard.

'You can't train with the team,' Danny told Tasha. 'Sidney might suspect something. But if you kick the ball around with Rachel and Sam I'll come along and give you a few tips.'

'Thanks, Danny,' said Tasha. She didn't mention that there might be some tips she could give him.

They trained in groups for dribbling and trapping; and in lines for spot kicks. Terry worked them hard in passing and positioning. Sidney came but watched for most of the time.

The gang knew that if their plan succeeded they stood a good chance of beating the Denby Flyers on Saturday. But after that . . . ? 'Don't think about it,' said Rachel. 'It's worth the risk.'

Tasha sat in her mum's car. Her dad had gone to Bigley to play for the Wanderers so her mum had given her a lift to the Dale Valley game. She wore a red tracksuit over her football gear and the butter-flies in her tummy were for real.

Rachel was at the entrance to the car park watching Simon. He was sitting on the bank at the side of the call box. Julie was in the club's office, keeping guard over the telephone.

Then the Rolls arrived. Mr Blinks drove into the car park as though he had royalty on the back seat. Rachel waved and saw Simon enter the box to make the call. Two minutes later, just as Mr Blinks was tying Sidney's trainers, Julie came running from the office.

'Sorry, Mr Blinks,' she said. 'A telephone call for you. The man says it's urgent. Something to do with Sidney.'

Mr Blinks ran into the club. Julie followed and listened at the office door.

'Yes, he's a good player and he knows a lot about the game,' he was saying. 'Rehearsal this afternoon and performance at 8.30 this evening? Good! I'll see you at the Bigley studio in about an hour.'

Mr Blinks stayed in the car park long enough to speak to the coach. 'Sorry, Terry,' he said. 'Sidney's been selected to appear on television. You'll have to find a replacement striker.'

Overhead a light aircraft swooped low across the pitch. It was towing a streamer that told everyone, in large red letters: 'Blinks Butter Biscuits are the Best.'

At the line-up Danny winked across at Tasha. 'We'll bury 'em,' he said.

But the Denby Flyers made a rapid start. Their midfield placed the ball in Dale Valley's half and, despite Mark's strong tackle, a striker ran clear to hammer the ball at the goal. It flew almost straight at Rob who fisted it brilliantly over the bar.

'We've got to get it in their half,' said Danny. He took the ball from Gary and raced towards the Flyer's goal. But their defenders closed in on him. He attempted to hook the ball to Tasha but he was too late. The ball was taken and booted back into Dale Valley's half.

Mark and Trev were on form. 'Good job we've got them back,' said Julie to Sam. He nodded. But the Flyers were desperate to get an early goal. Twice their strikers broke through Dale Valley's defence but each time Rob held the ball safely.

At half-time the score was 0–0.

'We're just not getting enough of the ball,' complained Tasha.

Terry agreed. 'Forget about fancy footwork,' he told the midfielders. 'Just keep booting long balls through the middle for our strikers to chase.'

This change in tactics surprised the Flyers' defenders. After a brilliant long ball from Kev in midfield Tasha took possession. She skirted around the defenders and hammered the ball into the corner of the net.

This was just the beginning of the best football Dale Valley had ever played. With powerful drives coming from their midfielders Tasha and Danny were getting a lot of the ball. The Flyers had put their strength into attacking but now, with Dale Valley on the offensive, they had to fall back and concentrate on their defence.

Tasha's second goal came from a brilliant header. A strong ball fired by Danny was returned to play by the Flyers' keeper. Tasha dived forward, cleverly avoiding a lunging defender, and placed the ball neatly over the line. Danny's goal, ten minutes later, came from an amazing show of determination. Taking a long ball from Kev he drove through the Flyers' midfield but finding the defenders bearing down on him he slid the ball to Tasha. She slotted it back immediately as the defenders came for her and Danny hammered it home, well beyond the keeper's reach.

The game finished with the score at 3–0. As the Dale Valley supporters broke on to the pitch Tasha leaned forward and kissed Danny on the cheek. 'You said we'd bury 'em,' she grinned.

On Monday most of the gang were playing table-tennis when Mr Blinks came into the room.

'This is it,' said Rachel to Danny. 'He's mad. He's closing us down.'

But Mr Blinks went over to Tasha. 'I've heard about you,' he said. 'You're our new top striker. Congratulations!'

He turned to Rachel. 'You're quite a player, too, I hear. I've just been telling Terry, it's time we had girls in the team.'

He raised his voice to speak to the gang. 'You know that Sidney and I were tricked into going to Bigley television studio on Saturday. But, no problem. We met the Desert Winds, the group at the top of the charts. Sidney's decided to give up football and learn the guitar. Show them your new gear, son.'

Sidney came into the room; purple trousers, a cream silk shirt and a guitar as big as himself.

'You know,' said Tasha to Rachel. 'I almost feel sorry for him. I'm glad my dad's not a millionaire.'

Seeing Red

ALAN DURANT

You know that feeling you get when they're doing the FA Cup draw on the telly and you're waiting for the ball with your team's number to be picked out? That nervy mixture of butterflies-in-the-stomach and excitement? Well, that's the way it was at Grafton Park's training session that Tuesday evening when the coach, Bill Davies, called the team together to announce who they were going to play in the quarter finals of the District Cup.

'Right,' said Bill. 'I know you're all dying to know who your next cup opponents will be.' His statement was met by a breathless hubbub. 'What do you want first: the good news or the bad news?'

'The good news!' Jamie Lewis responded quickly with the authority of the team captain that he was.

'Yes, the good news,' agreed Shanta, the team's star player, and other voices supported him.

'Okay,' said Bill, a smile on his round, healthily ruddy face. 'We'll be playing at home.'

'Yes!' cheered the team as one.

'And the bad news ...' Bill's smile became a grimace. 'We've been drawn against Barton.'

The response this time was more varied. Some groaned, some shrugged and one, Shanta, stood completely silent and still. When Jamie Lewis, who was standing next to him, turned towards his friend, Shanta's face was grim. It was as if he'd just heard that someone had died or something, not a cup draw.

'It'll be okay, Shanta,' Jamie said quietly. He put his hand on Shanta's shoulder. But Shanta shrugged it away.

'Barton,' he muttered glumly. 'Why of all teams did it have to be Barton?' He kicked up a divot of turf from the ground. Then, without another word, he turned and walked away.

It had been an excellent season so far for Grafton. They were currently top of their league, having won all but three of their matches, two of which had been drawn. Their only defeat had come at home and the team that had inflicted it upon them was Barton Green. The score had been 2–0, but the result told only half the story. For Shanta, the game had been a nightmare. Man marked throughout by a boy called Darren Powell, Shanta had hardly got a kick all match – well, a kick of the ball anyway; he'd had plenty of kicks on the legs and ankles, as well as jabs and shoves in the back, and all kinds of nasty threats and insults snarled in his ear. He'd come out of the game black and blue all over. But his tormentor had gone unpunished. Darren Powell was a thug but he was cunning too and had always committed his fouls on Shanta when the referee wasn't looking. A couple of times Shanta had complained, but the referee told him to get on with the game and stop moaning.

Finally, Shanta's temper had snapped. Reacting to a particularly painful dig in the ribs, Shanta had lashed out with his arm and caught Darren Powell full in the face with his elbow. Darren Powell had fallen to the ground as if shot. When Shanta turned, he saw his tormentor writhing on the ground with his hands over his face – and they were covered in blood. It had looked worse than it really was – Darren Powell just had a bleeding nose – but unfortunately for Shanta, on this occasion the referee *had* been looking. Without hesitation, he had reached into his pocket and shown Shanta the red card.

'Go on,' he'd said sternly. 'I've had enough of you. Get off.'

Shanta had raised his hands to protest, but, well, what could he say? Miserably, he'd trudged off the pitch and back to the changing rooms.

The score at the time had been nil all. But with almost all of the second half to go, Barton made their extra man count, netting two goals late in the game to win the match and deepen Shanta's misery. Most of his team-mates had witnessed Darren Powell's vicious tactics and after the match they were very sympathetic. No one blamed him for the loss. But Shanta blamed himself. He was angry and ashamed and very unhappy. He was in tears all the way home. Worse was to follow, though. Following the referee's report, the league organisers had charged Shanta with violent conduct and banned him for the rest of the season. Shanta was devastated, but Bill Davies had sent a letter appealing against the decision, and a number of spectators who had been at the match had supported him. The ban had been changed to three matches, but with a warning that if Shanta were sent off again, he would be banned from playing in the league for ever. Now Grafton had drawn Barton Green in the cup quarter finals, and, in the first game back after suspension, Shanta would have to face Darren Powell. No wonder he was feeling glum!

The evening after Bill Davies announced the draw, the Grafton Park coach turned up unexpectedly at Shanta's house.

'Sorry to disturb you, Mrs Nawaz,' he said with an apologetic smile. 'I just needed to have a little chat with Shanta about the match on Saturday. I expect he's told you we're playing Barton.'

Mrs Nawaz beckoned Bill Davies in. 'He's not said a word,' she said. 'He's been quiet as the grave since he got home last night. Now I know why.' She shook her head knowingly, then called upstairs to Shanta to come down.

'I'll leave you two to it,' she said when her son appeared, frowning, at the top of the stairs.

'Thanks,' said Bill. 'We won't be long.'

Shanta sat opposite his coach with a forlorn expression on his face.

'Cheer up,' Bill chided. 'You've got a cup quarter final on Saturday to look forward to.'

'Yes,' Shanta mumbled. 'Against Barton. And Darren Powell.'

'So?' the coach persisted. 'Barton are nothing special and Darren Powell's just a thug.'

'I know,' Shanta grumbled. 'I've still got a couple of bruises from last time we played.'

'You're not worried about a couple of bruises, are you?' said Bill lightly.

'No,' said Shanta.

'What is the matter, then?' asked Bill. 'Are you scared of Darren Powell? Is that it?'

Shanta snorted. 'Of course I'm not scared of him,' he rasped angrily. 'I'd stand up to that creep any day. I'd ...' He cut himself short, glancing guiltily at his raised fist.

'That's what I was afraid of,' sighed Bill. He looked at the boy with unusual severity. 'If you can't control your temper, Shanta, then I can't risk playing you. This match means too much to the team. I know what an important player you are – heaven knows we've missed you these last few games – but I think I'm going to have to leave you out of this one – for your own good and the team's.'

'No,' cried Shanta. 'You can't do that.'

'I can and I will,' said Bill firmly. His gaze softened a little. 'Look, Shanta, you're a very talented lad. You don't want to ruin your whole football career before it gets started for the sake of one football match – even if it is a quarter final. There'll be other quarter finals – and semi-finals, and finals too, hopefully. Why not give this one a miss?'

He looked searchingly at his young striker. It would be so easy to agree, thought Shanta – to drop out of this one; the team would still have a good chance of winning without him. And if they didn't, no one would blame him, would they? *Oh, yes they would*, a voice in his head replied. *You would blame yourself.*

Shanta looked down at the floor. 'I want to play,' he said softly. Then, lifting his head so that he was staring straight into the coach's keen blue eyes, he added beseechingly, 'Please.'

For several moments, the room was tensely silent, while Bill Davies contemplated the dilemma that faced him. Then, at last, his features relaxed into a half smile and he nodded. 'Okay, you're in. But,' he warned, 'one hint of trouble and I'm taking you off. Understood?'

'I won't make any trouble,' Shanta promised. Then he smiled for the first time that day. 'Well, except for the Barton defence. I'll give them plenty of trouble – trying to stop me scoring ...'

'That's the spirit,' said Bill Davies happily. 'Let your skill do the talking, not your fists.'

'Barton Green won't know what's hit them,' said Shanta and his smile broadened into a grin.

A few days later, lining up for the kick-off with Barton Green and seeing Darren Powell waiting for him, Shanta didn't feel quite so confident. He felt unusually nervous: he was excited about the game, yet almost wished it was over. And it didn't take long for Darren Powell to make his mark. The match was only minutes old when the Barton defender gave Shanta a sharp tap on the ankle that made him hop up in pain – but out of the referee's view of course.

'That's for last time,' Darren Powell hissed. 'No one hits me and gets away with it. You're really going to get it now.'

He nudged Shanta in the back, pushing him forward. Shanta stumbled then turned with a glare at his marker. His face was hot with anger.

'I'm not scared of you,' he said fiercely. He would have said more too, only he suddenly remembered Bill Davies's words. Glancing across at the touch line Shanta could see the coach staring across at him and the heavy frown on his face. Quickly, he moved away. It was fortunate that he did, too, because at that moment Jamie Lewis threaded a pass through towards him. Shanta took it and, finding himself in space for once, with Darren Powell metres away, he was able to turn and run at the Barton defence. In a flash he was past two flat-footed defenders and in the Barton penalty box. As the goalkeeper advanced to narrow the angle, Shanta dummied to shoot, then rolled the ball sideways for Jamie Lewis to run on to and thump first time into the back of the net. Goal! Less than five minutes gone and Grafton were one-nil up! Shanta was delighted. As he ran back to the centre circle, he passed Darren Powell, who scowled at him unpleasantly.

'That's the last touch of the ball you'll get,' he snarled.

Shanta just grinned and said nothing. He didn't need to. Well, his feet had done his talking for him, hadn't they? He'd shown Darren Powell who was boss.

'Great run, Shanta,' Jamie Lewis congratulated him. 'Thanks for the pass. I thought you were going to shoot yourself.'

'Well, maybe I will next time,' said Shanta happily. He'd get another chance soon, he was sure of that.

But his confidence was misplaced. Darren Powell may not have been the most skilful footballer on the pitch, but he was a strong defender – and he was as good as his word: for the rest of the first half, Shanta hardly touched the ball. Every time a pass was hit in his direction, Darren Powell intercepted it or tackled Shanta before he had the chance to get the space to move away. And in between times, when the referee wasn't looking, he used his full range of dirty tricks to try to hurt and provoke Shanta. The names he called him were even nastier now and Shanta was finding it more and more difficult to control his temper. He was just a step away from lashing out.

It wasn't just Shanta personally who was struggling. After their glorious start, Grafton started to lose their way and allow Barton back in the game. A careless mistake in their defence let Barton's central striker, Carl Hewitt, race clear to shoot home the equaliser. Even worse, in his brave attempt to save the goal, Grafton's keeper, Danny Marsden, landed heavily and injured himself.

'I think he's dislocated his shoulder,' Bill Davies announced glumly, as Danny was led away in tears by one of the watching parents to be taken to hospital. 'He certainly won't be taking any further part in this match.'

Grafton had a substitute, Jermain Stewart, but he wasn't a goalkeeper, so Bill Davies had to reorganise the team. Shanta's fellow striker, Mark Bridges, the tallest player in the side, went in goal and Jermain took his place up front. It wasn't a happy arrangement. With Shanta shackled by Darren Powell and Grafton's midfield passing badly, Jermain was unable to get into the game at all – while at the back, Mark Bridges had a nightmare.

In the space of three minutes at the end of the first half, Mark had let in two goals. The first, a rocket of a shot from Barton's captain, Ben Smith, wasn't his fault, but the second definitely was. Carl Hewitt's soft header seemed to be bouncing harmlessly into the stand-in keeper's hands, but somehow, Mark Bridges let it slip through. To the horror of the watching Grafton players, the ball trickled over the line for a goal. At half-time Grafton were 3–1 down and staring defeat in the face.

Bill Davies was furious.

'Don't you want to get into the semi-final?' he stormed. 'You're throwing the game away.' Brusquely, he listed the many things the team was doing wrong. His most stinging remarks were saved for Shanta.

'It's no good just waiting for the ball to come to you, Shanta, and letting Darren Powell say "thank you very much" as he takes it off you,' said the coach severely. 'You've got to move about. Make space.'

'But how can I make space?' Shanta grumbled. 'Everywhere I go, Darren Powell follows. Look at my legs.' He rolled down the sock on his right leg to reveal a collection of bruises.

Bill Davies shook his head. 'If I had another substitute I'd take you off,' he said. 'But I don't.' He gave Shanta a searching look. 'But if you really haven't got the stomach to cope with a marker, then maybe you should swap with Mark and take his place in goal. Let's see how he gets on against Darren Powell.'

Mark Bridges' face lit up at this suggestion. After his error in the first-half, he had no wish to stay in goal. It was a tempting offer too, Shanta had to admit. He couldn't do worse than Mark had done and he'd be free of Darren Powell at last. But just at that instant, he caught a glimpse of the Barton boy, leering across at him triumphantly – and Shanta's anger rose. He couldn't let Darren Powell think he'd beaten him. He had to stay out on the field.

'I'll move about,' he said sharply. 'Darren Powell will have to run a marathon to stay with me.'

'Good,' said Bill Davies. 'Take him all over the field, test his stamina. And if you still can't shake him off, then come deeper, into your own half and let Jamie push on up front. I'll give you the sign. Okay?'

'Okay,' said Shanta. Then it was time to line up for the second-half.

As the Grafton players jogged to their positions, the coach put a hand on Shanta's arm. 'Remember, Shanta,' he said quietly, 'keep your anger in your feet. Hit Barton where it really hurts – in their goal.'

'I'll try,' Shanta promised. But trying wasn't enough, he knew: he had to succeed.

Grafton started the second half as they had the first, with some good, flowing attacks, going close to scoring on two occasions. Then, at last, they got their reward when Jamie Lewis tapped in his second goal following a corner. Shanta, however, still couldn't get into the game. He moved from wing to wing to try and find space, but he couldn't shake off his marker. All he got for his trouble were a couple more bruises. Darren Powell was starting to breath quite heavily now, though, and no longer had the puff to utter his insults, which encouraged Shanta to carry on with his running.

'I've got you now,' he said to himself.

But Darren Powell was nothing if not determined. His breathing got more and more laboured yet he wouldn't let Shanta escape his clutches – and his off-the-ball tricks got more vicious. As Grafton attacked down their right side, Shanta moved to sprint towards the centre from the position he'd taken up out on the left wing. He'd barely taken two steps, though, when his legs were swept from under him and he collapsed to the ground.

'Ah!' he cried, clutching his left ankle, which had twisted in the fall.

'Had a nice trip?' sneered Darren Powell, standing over him. The Barton boy's taunting words and expression made Shanta see red. A jolt of anger surged through him.

'You dirty thug!' he hissed, lifting his foot to kick

out … It was the sound of his coach's voice, calling from the nearby touch-line, that stopped him. Shanta dropped his leg and, gingerly, got up on his feet.

'Shanta!' Bill Davies called again. Glancing aside, Shanta saw his coach jerk a thumb in the direction of the Grafton half. Shanta nodded, then, limping slightly, he trotted away from his marker, who watched him with a look of hard satisfaction. This time, he didn't bother trying to follow.

There were barely ten minutes of the match left now. Grafton were trying hard, but their early second-half pressure had eased through tiredness. The Barton players were weary too but they kept on battling with everyone back behind the ball. Only something special, it seemed, could unlock their defence – and Shanta was the one to provide it. Taking the ball from Mark Bridges, deep in his own half, he sprinted forward. As a man, the Barton side fell back before him and he was able to get half-way into his opponents' half before someone came to challenge him. Shanta swerved past him and quickly eased by a second tackle too. There were still plenty of Barton players between him and the goal, though.

As Shanta looked up to see who was free in front of him, Jamie Lewis made a darting run across the penalty box towards him. Shanta shaped as if to pass to him, but held on to the ball instead, moving inside towards the Barton goal. Two Barton defenders had gone with Jamie Lewis, expecting him to get the ball and, now, suddenly, a gap had opened in the heart of the Barton defence. Shanta needed no second invitation. Quick as a flash, he was through the gap and bearing down on the Barton goal. Unsure whether to come or stay, the Barton keeper dithered and by the time he'd made up his mind to advance it was too late. Shanta had slipped the ball past him and into the corner of the net. Grafton had equalised! It was 3–3. Shanta slid to the ground in delight, as his team-mates ran to congratulate him.

'Great goal, son!' Bill Davies shouted from the touch line, his round face ruddier than ever. 'Now, let's have another one!'

Shanta did his best to oblige. In the next few minutes he got more good touches of the ball than he'd had in the whole game up till then. Twice he set up clear chances for his team-mates with clever runs and passes, but each time they failed to make them count. As if gathering confidence from their good fortune, Barton mounted one last attack and won a corner. As he trotted over to take the kick, Ben Smith waved his team-mates forward. The Grafton penalty area was a mass of Barton green and Grafton blue. Only the Barton goalkeeper remained in his own half of the field. The kick came over. Jermain Stewart got his head to the ball but only knocked it up in the air. Darren Powell leapt high and headed the ball back hopefully towards the Grafton goal – and there was Carl Hewitt unmarked, on the edge of the six-yard box! It seemed that he must score ... But no! Bravely, Mark Bridges flung himself forward to smother the ball just as the striker was about to shoot.

'Brilliant save!' cried Jamie Lewis. While all eyes turned towards the Barton goalkeeper, Shanta made his move.

'Mark!' he shouted. 'Kick it!' Then he turned and ran upfield. Mark Bridges' kick was a good one. Making full use of his striker's skills, he thumped the ball well into the Barton half. Shanta was away. His first touch, though, took him a little to one side of the field and by the time he'd got the ball under control and got back on course, he was aware of a figure snapping at his heels. Somehow he knew at once, even without seeing him, who it was: Darren Powell. Shanta accelerated forward, making sure he didn't push the ball too far ahead of him. Darren Powell followed doggedly. He may have been tired but he wasn't going to let his quarry go free.

Shanta was in the penalty area now, the Barton keeper coming out to meet him. Darren Powell was at his shoulder. Should he shoot now, even though the angle was bad, and hope for the best, or . . . ? He stopped and swivelled with the ball. Darren Powell was completely fooled. He ran right past Shanta, who came back inside and advanced on the goal. A shimmy left, then right and the keeper was out of it, lying helplessly on the turf. The goal was at Shanta's mercy. He pulled back his foot to tap home the ball and whack! For the second time in the match his legs were swept from under him by Darren Powell. This time, though, the incident had happened in full view of the referee. Instantly, he blew his whistle and pointed to the penalty spot. Then, beckoning to Darren Powell with one hand, he reached into his pocket with the other. Picking himself up, Shanta watched as Darren Powell was shown the red card and sent from the pitch.

'That'll teach him, dirty fouler,' Jermain muttered. 'He should have been off ages ago.'

Shanta said nothing. The job was not yet complete. Coolly, he picked up the ball and placed it on the penalty spot. Then he turned and took a few steps back. The Barton keeper swayed nervously on his line. The whistle blew. Shanta stood motionless for an instant, then trotted forward and thump! The ball was in the net: 4–3! Grafton had beaten Barton with the last kick of the quarter final! As his teammates leapt and whooped for joy, Shanta looked across to the changing rooms, into which Darren Powell was about to disappear, and he raised a fist in the air. Returning his gaze to the pitch, all he could see was the rush of blue that swiftly enveloped him.

Tanner's Ace

PETER DIXON

Jason placed his Inter-Milano sports bag on the spare seat and settled down for the drive to Fern End Middle School. He knew they had a poor side and looked forward to scoring his third hat-trick of the season. Being captain he swiftly bagged the front seat, and hoped that Thalia Mansell would notice the scarlet Inter-Milano shirt draped across his shoulders. No one else possessed a Milan shirt, and no one else had a photograph of themselves scoring the winning goal for the district side.

He slipped the picture from the back page of the gazette into his hand and gazed at it once again. Surely Thalia must have seen it? Perhaps she had even cut it out and pinned it to her wall. His head spun at the thought. Thalia, the best-looking girl in the school – perhaps she really had cut out her own copy. He reread the caption printed in large, fat, black letters:

TANNER'S ACE
Local boy

He didn't want to grin but couldn't quite help it. Tanner's ace. Yes, that's what he was – an ace. The best sportsman in the school.

Even at the pre-school playgroup he had won more races than anyone else, and this success had continued throughout his infant and junior years. Now, aged eleven, he was still winning just about everything he entered, and if it hadn't been for stupid Porky Day he would have won the young Athlete of the Year award at the area sports. Stupid, giggling, silly Porky Day who had tripped him at the very first bend of the 400 metres, and even Jason couldn't win a race with only one shoe and a bleeding knee. Stupid, bloomin' Porky Day, tripping someone up was typical of him. Just the sort of daft thing he would do. Jason turned his head towards the back seat where Porky and Mickey Iddon were wrestling each other. Porky had pulled his football bag over Iddon's head, and Iddon had trapped Porky's head between his elbow and the back of the seat. There were a lot of muffled hissings and groanings, mixed with outbursts of giggles and grunts. Their battle was attracting considerable attention and with some dismay, Jason noticed that Thalia and some of the other girls seemed to be enjoying the struggle and even encouraging the pair to wrestle harder.

For a moment Jason considered informing Mr Pike of the foolish behaviour in the back seat, but noticing the furrowed ridges of concentration upon their teacher's brow, he decided that perhaps it wasn't a wise move. Mr Pike needed all his concentration for the road. At least Thalia had decided to come and support the team and Jason secretly hoped that he was the main attraction. But whatever could she find amusing about Porky Day? Porky was a twit and why had Mr Pike put him in the squad anyway, Jason wondered? He didn't even own a designer sports bag and in their previous match he had worn a pair of his brother's old army cadet boots. One of them seemed devoid of laces and every time Porky attempted a left-footed clearance, the boot flew off and sailed high into the air and he had to scramble after it.

And then there was the incident of the shredded shirt. Porky had snatched Iddon's number seven shirt from his bag in one of their usual struggles and thrown it into the caretaker's front garden. Before Mickey could retrieve it, Mr Lambercraft's basset hound and a mongrel which hung around the kitchens had torn it to shreds in a battle of snarls, snaps and writhing bodies. There was a terrible row. Mr Pike had ordered Porky to give his shirt to Mickey Iddon and poor Porky had had to play in his vest. It was a particularly nasty vest of a sort of fluffy ivory colour, but Porky didn't care and laughed as loudly as anyone else when Frankie Burrows pointed out huge holes down the side and the massive brown iron stain in the middle of the back.

The thought of playing in a grandfather vest in front of fifty supporters including the glorious Thalia filled Jason with sickening horror, but Porky hadn't cared a jot. It was in that same match that

Iddon and Porky had used some of the half-time orange peel to make themselves goofy teeth and upset the referee. Jason had reported them to Mr Pike, who in turn relegated them to the role of substitutes for the next two games.

'Football is a serious game and a pitch is no place for fooling,' Mr Pike had announced. Jason had felt pleased. He was secretly delighted to know that they wouldn't be starting the match today.

The mini-bus gave a lurch as it negotiated two linked roundabouts, and Jason's new bag slipped sideways. He stared at it with pleasure. No one else in the entire county owned a scarlet Inter-Milano bag, it was unique.

Yet he remembered, not for the first time, that this wasn't true: Glenda had one. Silly, squealy Glenda. She had one and to Jason it didn't seem fair. It was bad enough having a nearly six foot elder sister, but her ownership of an Inter-Milano sports bag was impossible for Jason to accept.

When their Uncle Derek had visited the factory in Italy where they were made, he had brought two back. Why two? One bag would have been perfect. Why hadn't he brought Glenda something different? She didn't even play football, in fact she didn't play anything much. Majorettes, that was her thing, and every time Jason observed her folding her white skirt, blouse, knickers and bra into a soft little bundle and placing them in her bag with an assortment of lucky koala bears, pretty towels and stepping boots, he wanted to scream. Inter-Milano bags were not designed for sisters who marched round in high stepping parades of long legs, batons and swirling skirts, they were for football stars. People such as himself and other guys. Every time Jason saw her bag he felt like kicking it as far as ...

There was a scream! It was followed by a cry from Thalia, and Mr Pike hit the brakes. It was Iddon's voice trumpeting through the mini-bus.

'It's Perkins, sir. Perkins is being sick, sir. Perkins is being sick all over!' And so he was. Perkins stood grey as sugar paper amidst a host of scrabbling travellers and tumbling sports bags, spurting a deluge of pink froth.

'It's sherbet!' screamed Julie Davis, trying to hide beneath her seat. 'It's sherbet sick.'

Amidst the shrieking and chaos, Jason fought to drag his bag from Perkins's range but it was too late.

Then as suddenly as he started, Perkins stopped. For a moment he looked vaguely puzzled and then he sat down and wiped his mouth on his cuff.

'It was Porky Day who done it,' shouted Neil. 'Me and Thalia heard him daring Perkins to eat those five packets all at once. He said he'd give him a set of England cards if he did,' he added. There was a further silence, even the road was empty and quiet.

'Everyone out,' snapped Mr Pike,' and keep away from the road.'

They sat on a low white wall which surrounded the garden of a big posh house, whilst Mr Pike dished out wads of green paper towels and people dabbed each other off. It was horrible. Jason's Inter-Milano bag seemed to have caught the worst of the mess and he was moaning and groaning whilst attempting to remove the foaming fluid with half a packet of green paper towels. Only Perkins seemed at all cheerful and wandered around with a smile telling everyone how much better he felt.

Mr Pike was obviously terribly angry and had begun making an announcement about telephoning the school, when Danny La Rocca appeared. Mr Pike noticed the man as he waved from the gravel path leading to the double garage, nosed by a bright silver sports car and a Mercedes. For a moment he thought it was a grumpy rich man complaining about schoolchildren sitting on his wall.

He couldn't have been more wrong! As the bronzed figure strode forward Iddon gave a whoop of recognition. It was Rovers' leading goal scorer and international superstar, Danny La Rocca himself! The class fell into silence. Jason ceased dabbing his bag, and even Mr Pike looked embarrassed and tongue-tied. It didn't matter, though, for Danny had everything under control.

At a glance, he noted the array of football gear, Perkins clutching the yellow bucket and Jason still dabbing his bag. Danny groaned. He was bigger, browner and even more wonderful than anyone ever imagined. He had a tattoo on the hairy part of his wrist and a gold medallion around his neck.

'It happens to the best of us,' he laughed, patting Perkins' head. 'But where are you off to?'

'Fern End School,' Mr Pike replied. 'Can we use your phone – I'll have to cancel.'

'Cancel!' roared Danny, his gold filling glinting. 'Cancel! We don't cancel matches as important as yours, do we Jack?'

A small man holding a rake had appeared at his side. Danny looked at his watch.

'Fern End School's five miles from here. I'll drive ahead and tell them you're delayed and when you've cleaned things up a bit you can drive on.'

Mr Pike opened his mouth and shut it again.

'Well, who's coming in the advance party with me?' Danny grinned.

Of course, everyone wanted to say 'Me.' The idea of driving into Fern End School with Danny La Rocca in a sports car was a dream come true – yet only Jason spoke.

'I'll come,' he said very coolly. 'I'm the captain and I know the way.'

'And me!' cried Porky Day. 'I'll sit in the back.'

He moved towards the driveway, but Jason moved faster.

'No, not you, Porky! I think one of the girls. How about Thalia?'

'Okay, one of each sounds about right' said Danny, laughing, and he vaulted the garden gate and trotted towards the car.

The moment the sports car swept into the Fern End School playground with Jason seated beside Danny La Rocca was the greatest moment of his eleven and a half years. Thalia's hair had blown in the breeze for the entire journey and on one occasion she had leaned so far forward that their cheek's had almost touched. Jason had half-turned – grinned, and sensed that she had enjoyed the contact as much as he had himself.

Within minutes Danny La Rocca was recognised. News sped through the school and a crowd of Lower Juniors followed the trio towards the pitch, waving, pointing and chanting the Rovers' song. Danny grinned and Jason waved. They explained the situation to the Fern End School's teacher who understood the dilemma and agreed to postpone the kick-off for a short while, and then when Danny agreed to stay and watch the match for a few minutes, the day was completed.

'Perhaps you'd like me to be photographed shaking hands with the two captains,' he suggested.

Thalia laughed and asked if he could also play on her side.

'We could chuck out Iddon and have a decent striker,' joked Jason, throwing his arm across Thalia's shoulder and beaming to all those standing near. The time flew as magic minutes always do, and suddenly Jason realised that his team were trotting on to the pitch, having changed in the mini-bus.

A moment of panic struck him. 'My bag! Quick! I must change! Where's my bag?'

'You left it on the wall,' said Mr Pike rather grumpily. 'But don't worry, we brought it for you.'

Without a word Jason grabbed the bag and fled to the changing room. He tore off his shoes, socks, jacket and shirt and unzipped the chrome Inter-Milano double-way siliconed zipper. He pulled away the towel covering the kit and stared down. A pair of neatly folded knickers, a bra, blouse and silver-tipped majorette cane stared back.

'Hurry up!' called Mr Pike. 'The *Gazette* want a picture of you shaking hands with Mr La Rocca!'